Come Back to the 5 & Dime, Jimmy Dean, Jimmy Dean

A Comedy–Drama

by Ed Graczyk

A SAMUEL FRENCH ACTING EDITION

SAMUEL FRENCH

FOUNDED 1830

New York Hollywood London Toronto

SAMUELFRENCH.COM

ISBN   978-0-573-60764-6   Printed   in   U.S.A.   #5147

"Come Back to the 5 & Dime, Jimmy Dean, Jimmy Dean" was first produced by Players Theatre of Columbus, Ohio in September, 1976 and directed by the author. It was subsequently produced by the Alliance Theatre Company, Atlanta, Georgia in February, 1977, directed by Fred Chappell. The original New York production was directed by Barbara Loden and David Kerry Heefner at the Hudson Guild Theatre in February, 1980. The Broadway production, directed by Robert Altman, opened February 18, 1982 at the Martin Beck Theatre. This script is a combination of the Off-Broadway and Broadway productions.

OPENING NIGHT — February 18, 1982

MARTIN BECK THEATRE

OWNED AND OPERATED BY JUJAMCYN THEATERS
RICHARD G. WOLFF, PRESIDENT

DAN FISHER   JOSEPH CLAPSADDLE   JOEL BRYKMAN

and

JACK LAWRENCE

present

SANDY   CHER   KAREN
DENNIS   BLACK

A new play by
ED GRACZYK

also starring

KATHY BATES   MARTA HEFLIN

and

SUDIE BOND

with

MARK PATTON

Scenic Design by	Costume Design by	Lighting Design by	Sound Design by
DAVID GROPMAN	SCOTT BUSHNELL	PAUL GALLO	RICHARD FITZGERALD

Casting Director and Assistant to the Director
SCOTT BUSHNELL

Directed by
ROBERT ALTMAN

ORIGINAL N Y PRODUCTION BY THE HUDSON GUILD THEATRE
DAVID KERRY HEEFNER, PRODUCING DIRECTOR

The Producers and Theatre Management are Members
of The League of New York Theatres and Producers, Inc.

CAST

(in order of appearance)

Juanita .... SUDIE BOND

Sissy .... CHER

Mona .... SANDY DENNIS

Joe .... MARK PATTON

Sue Ellen .... GENA RAMSEL

Stella May .... KATHY BATES

Edna Louise .... MARTA HEFLIN

Martha .... ANN RISLEY

Alice Ann .... DIANNE TURLEY TRAVIS

Clarissa .... RUTH MILLER

Joanne .... KAREN BLACK

CAST

JUANITA

MONA

MONA (THEN)

SISSY

SISSY (THEN)

JOE

JOANNE

STELLA MAY

EDNA LOUISE

TIME

SEPTEMBER 30, 1975
SEPTEMBER 30, 1955

PLACE

A FIVE-AND-DIME IN McCARTHY,
A SMALL TOWN IN WEST TEXAS

THE SET

The H.L. Kressmont Company is one of a small chain of nickel and dime emporiums struggling for survival in small out-of-touch towns throughout Texas. This particular store has existed since the late twenties and to this day has been virtually ignored by time, and change.

Upstage in the main wall, elevated by several steps, are large crowded windows of sun-bleached merchandise, through which can barely be seen the outside world. Between the two windows are double swinging screen doors. Wooden doors with glass inserts stand open with green window shades at half mast. Dirty white globes hang from the suggestion of a decorative pressed-metal ceiling, along with a large blade fan. A lunch counter is stage right with several swivel stools in front. Near the counter are two small tables with four chairs crowded around each. Behind the counter are limited cooking facilities and a section of wall boasting one of those paintings on glass that light up of the "Last Supper." Directly beneath it hangs the meager menu, and surrounding it, several tacked up advertisements for Dr. Pepper, Alka-Seltzer, etc. Black-crusted coils of flypaper dangle over the counter and the covered dishes of cakes and doughnuts. A beat-up Orange Crush machine churns and gurgles away on the upstage end of the counter.

Stage left is a curtained door leading into a section of the back storage room. Stacked boxes and crowded shelves isolate a small playing area, beyond which is a restroom, and additional storage space.

There is a comic book rack with a bench in front, a pay telephone, gum ball machine and several potted plants on stands that hang limp from the heat. A glass transom over the doors proclaims the existence of the "H.L. Kressmont Co." in the same lettering style that identifies five-and-dime stores all over the country.

The walls of the store are crowded with framed photographs, magazine covers and memorabilia of James Dean. A small table around which most of the photos center acts as a shrine. The center photo is framed with a string of Christmas tree lights that can be turned on by a switch. There is also hung a gawdy gold plaque awarded the employees of the store for outstanding sales, and a photograph of the original "Disciples of James Dean."

The store is in the process of being decorated for the twentieth reunion of the "Disciples." Twirled and swagged overhead are streamers of black crepe paper and decorations from holidays past; a Santa Claus head, red paper bells,

Halloween skeleton, Thanksgiving turkey, etc. A crudely painted sign hangs above proclaiming the event: "The 20th Anniversary Reunion of the Disciples of James Dean, September 30, 1955— September 30, 1975." Several streamers still dangle without connection near a ladder and cardboard box of more decorations.

ACT I

(*The store sags motionless with only the sound of the gurgling Orange Crush machine until moments before the house lights begin to dim, softly at first, seeping from the innards of the store, is heard the overture to "Giant." The music builds in volume as it travels forward to engulf the audience with its majestic movie impression of Texas. As the lights dim to darkness the music fades to underscore the opening scene. A light comes up behind the screen doors on JUANITA, the manager of the store. Her hair is attractively styled, but obviously the result of a home permanent. She wears a simple housedress, kitchen apron and comfortable shoes. SHE shields her eyes from the sun as she searches the street.*)

JUANITA. Jimmy Dean?...Jimmy Dean?!...You come back here to the five-and-dime now. Jimmy Dean. (*The phone rings and the lights come up inside the store.*) Jimmy Dean, are you hearin' me? (*SHE mutters to herself as SHE goes to the phone.*) His mother's gonna die a thousan' deaths when her bus comes pullin' on in an' he's no where to be found. (*Answers the phone.*) Kressmont five-and-dime, Juanita talkin'...Who?...I can't hardly hear you... Stella May?!...Well, where are ya talkin' from,

9

the moon?...Oh...Well, we got your letter just day before yesterday...ain't nothin' gone wrong now, has it?...You're still comin' to Mona's reunion party ain't ya?...Good...good...Mona would be real heart-sick not to have you here. No, no, she went over to Marfa this weekend...her bus is nearly two hours late in gettin' back...Sure hope there ain't been no...What?...She goes there every year 'bout this time to get together with all them others who was in that movie with her (SHE *hears the bus coming down the street.*) Wait...wait, I think I hear her bus pullin' in now, if you want to hang on...All right then...fine...fine, I'll tell her. You drive careful now, you hear...and tell Edna Louise we're all lookin' forward to seein' her too...now, you don't pick on her like that, you hear?...Bye, see you real soon.

(*During the above a fly has been annoying her.* SHE *goes behind the counter for her fly swatter and stations herself in wait.* SHE *notices the "Last Supper" picture isn't lit and pulls the string.* MONA *appears at the door.* SHE *is in her late thirties and wears a simple shirtwaist dress and low heels.* SHE *carries a purse, small beat-up suitcase and a paperback copy of "Gone With The Wind." The long bus ride and horrible heat show their effects on her. The built up anxiety of the reunion along with the haunting memories churned-up during the trip to Marfa has caused her to become restless and high-strung.*)

MONA. (*Ruffled*) That darn-fool of a bus broke down out there in the middle of nowhere and it took them nearly forever to get it repaired. Look at me ... would you just take a look at me, I'm a shambles ... an absolute shambles.

JUANITA. Come sit yourself down and let me fix you a nice cold Orange Crush. You do look like somethin' the cat mighta dragged in.

MONA. (*Pulling her dress away from her sticky body.*) Isn't this heat somethin' terrible though? My clothes are just stickin' to my body like glue. (*Fanning herself.*) We were forced to sit out there in that desolute emptiness in that broken down old bus for nearly four hours ... four hours in this oppressin' heat.

JUANITA. Two.

MONA. What?

JUANITA. Two hours. It was only two hours.

MONA. (*Laughs.*) Well, it seemed more like four. (*Suddenly remembers.*) Sandwiches ... did anybody remember about sandwiches?

JUANITA. Sissy's gone by to pick up the fixin's ... all we gotta do is put 'em together ... just calm yourself down.

MONA. (*A sigh of relief.*) Well thank heavens *that* worry can be erased from my mind. (*Takes a deep breath.*) It's so hot an' suffocatin' I can hardly hold a breath. (SHE *switches on the lights around the photo of Dean.*) Where's Jimmy Dean?

JUANITA. He ran off sometime after lunch an' I haven't seen hide nor hair of him since ...

MONA. Juanita, somethin' awful coulda happened

to him and you'd never know about it.

JUANITA. (*Irritated.*) Ain't nothin' happened to that boy, awful or otherwise ... He's prob'ly just over to Luke's Texaco watchin' him work on the cars or somethin'.

MONA. You know how I hafta worry about ...

JUANITA. You worry about him entirely too much ... now, drink this here Orange Crush an' cool yourself down. He's a big boy an' can take care of himself.

MONA. (*Laughs.*) Well, *that's* not a true remark and you very-well know it. (SHE *chuckles.*) My, that really does hit the spot. He shouldn't be runnin' aroun' out there in this heat though, he could get himself sun-stroke. (*Looks up.*) I sure wish that poor old broken ceilin' fan up there could see its way to start spinnin' again in time for tonight's party.

JUANITA. Sissy's stoppin' over to see if Luke'll come on by an' take a look at it ... although I don't know what good it would do even if he could get it to spinnin' again.

MONA. It's prob'ly just too hot an' tired to move.

JUANITA. Aren't you even gonna mention the decorations?

MONA. (*Startled.*) Good heavens, I neglected to even notice. (SHE *rushes down to get the full view.*) My, would you just look how this place has been all gussied up ... and what a clever idea to use the holidays as a way of showin' the passin' of the years.

JUANITA. Sissy worked all day long practic'ly, stringin' that stuff up there ...

MONA. (*Rushes to* JUANITA.) Are you as excited and nervous as I am? I could hardly contain myself the whole week-end long in Marfa just thinkin' about it. (*Studying the sign.*) Twenty years tonight ... seems like only yesterday, doesn't it ... when that fatal crash took away his life.

JUANITA. Lord, I nearly forgot, Stella May called-up just as your bus was pullin' in to say she's stopped off over in Odessa to give Edna Louise a ride ... just as quick as Edna can close-up the Beauty Parlor, they'll be on their way.

MONA. (*Excited.*) Won't it be wonderful to see them again ... Stella seem like she's changed any to you?

JUANITA. Her *voice* sounded much the same as it did back then ... an' she was pickin'-away at Edna same as before.

MONA. Anybody else call you an' say they was comin'?

JUANITA. 'fraid not.

MONA. Maybe they're intendin' to surprise us ... do ya think?

JUANITA. Don't get your heart too set on ...

MONA. I sent them little reminder notes to everyone askin' them to R.S.V.P.

JUANITA. It's been twenty years ... things change.

MONA. (SHE *goes to the group photo of the Disciples.*) I certainly hope we'll all be able to recognize each other ... wouldn't that be awful? (*Putting down the photo.*) I'm sure they'll all remember ... how could they possibly have forgotten such a devoted promise as that. (SHE *turns to see a figure standing behind the screen door. It is a young boy (Joe) looking like a vision of an angel with the pale look of vulnerable innocence. His face is soft and delicate with eyes like a wounded animal.* HE *wears a short-sleeved shirt, faded denim overalls and high-top black tennis shoes looking ever so much like James Dean in "East of Eden."* MONA *turns away from him quickly losing a breath.*)

JUANITA. You all right?

MONA. It seems like my heart just skipped a beat or somethin' (SHE *turns again. The figure has disappeared.*) ... it's just all this dry air I guess, affectin' my asthma somethin' awful.

JUANITA. (*Going to the counter.*) Now, you come set over here an' drink some more of this Orange Crush. It'll do wonders to cool off your insides.

MONA. I don't think I'll be able to sit again for a week or more. (*Rubs her backside.*) It seems that bus ride gets longer and longer every year. Either that or I'm gettin' older and less tolerable. (SHE *starts to drink but is interrupted by something that makes her laugh.*) Alice Marie ... you remember Alice Marie from over in Waco? ... She says I remind her of Scarlett O'Hara. Isn't that an odd thing to say though? (*Laughs.*)

JUANITA. (*Tracking a fly with her swatter.*) Why on earth would she say somethin' like that?

MONA. Well, I suppose it's because that's who I remind her of. She says Reata is my Tara and James Dean is my Clark Gable. (*Smiles as* SHE *picks up the copy of the novel and flips through it.*) I never had given that a thought before but you know, it really is an interesting coincidence.

JUANITA. You find yourself some silly kinda coincidence in everythin'. You an' that Scarlett O'Hara are about as similar as me an' Jean Harlow. (SHE *swats a fly.*) Aha!

MONA. (*Moves up to the door.*) Well, Alice Marie discovered a resemblance.

JUANITA. It's all that movie watchin' ... an' book readin' that puts them ideas in your head, if you ask me.

MONA. Bein' deprived of a formal college education the way I was ... because of an affliction of which I had no control if I may again remind you ... I have been forced to investigate on my own the mysteries of the universe or become totally ignorant of life like everybody else in this town ... present company excluded, of course. I have managed to save my life from becomin' merely an existence with an aid of the novel-of-the-month club and the motion picture industry, of which I am totally indebted.

JUANITA. (*Heading toward the back room.*) Church goin' an' Bible readin' would have done you a whole lot better good.

MONA. You are well aware of my religious feelin's.

JUNITA. (*Stepping into the back room.*) You have none.

MONA. (*Moving down to the shrine.*) Precisely, the Lord turned his back on me at a very crucial time in my early life, causin' scars that will never heal.

JUANITA. (*In the back room.*) You can't blame the Lord for what ...

MONA. (*Moves up to the screen doors.*) I can ...

and I do! (*From outside, a young female voice calls out.*)

MONA (THEN). Juanita! (*The lights begin to change focus, altering the look of the store.*)

JUANITA. (*Sticking her head through the curtains and gestures toward the shrine.*) The blame belongs to that face there hangin' all over these walls ... It was him, not the Lord, who put all them foolhardy notions in your young head.

MONA (THEN). Juanita!

MONA. At that time of our lives he was our savior ... the only one who understood us. (SHE *goes outside. The sound of thunder and rain. The fan starts spinning and the lights have transformed the store dramatically to September* 30, 1955.)

JUANITA. Don't you just walk away from me like that, young lady.

(MONA (THEN) *appears in the doorway.* SHE *is seventeen and wears a mid-calf school dress of the fifties, anklets and saddle shoes. Her hair is long and in a pony tail. She carries a beat-up suitcase. As we move into the past,* JUANITA *remains the same, but twenty years earlier.*)

MONA (THEN). (*Excited.*) Juanita, I'm back! Aren't you surprised?! (*Laughs.*)

JUANITA. (*Going to her. Surprised.*) Mona! ... Lord, child, what are you doin' back here, already? We just waved you off to that college not more than a week ago.

MONA (THEN). I don't have to go after all ... Isn't that wonderful?

JUANITA. Don't have to go? What in heaven's name went wrong? (MONA, *behind the screen door, watches the scene in shadow.*)

MONA (THEN). My asthma. It got worse, it really did. That climate there was not right for my asthma. The Doctor said so.

JUANITA. They had to send for a doctor?

MONA (THEN). It was terrible. It really was. I was standin' in line waitin' to sign up for my classes when I just collapsed in a dead heap on the floor. It was real scary to everybody. They told me so afterwards ... They all thought I was dead or somethin'. (*Rushes and hugs* JUANITA.) Oh, I'm so excited to be back home with everybody. I was a fool to think I could ever leave here. Sidney will give me my job back, won't he?

JUANITA. (*Stunned.*) I'm sure he will.

MONA (THEN). (*Moving to a photo of Dean.*) How lucky for me it happened in time to return for tonight's meetin' of the "Disciples." I was real worried how the club would continue without my leadership. (*All smiles.*) Oh, I just missed everybody so very much. (*Quickly.*) Where's Sissy? ... and Joe? ... I can't wait to see their faces when they hear I'm back to stay. (*The lights begin to return to 1975. The thunder and rain fade. The fan stops.*)

JUANITA. Sissy's in the back room unpackin' some ...

MONA (THEN). (*Grabs her suitcase.*) I brought them back a surprise I can't wait to show 'em ... It's a whole entire magazine devoted to James Dean ... they'll just die when they see it ... (*Rushes to the back room.*)

JUANITA. Mona, honey, Joe's not ...

MONA (THEN). Sissy! ... Sissy ... Joe, I'm back.
(SHE *disappears into the back room.* JUANITA *starts
to follow but is stopped by* MONA)

MONA. (*Through the screen.*) Juanita, I apologize
for losin' my temper to you like that.

JUANITA. It's just as much my fault as yours
I suppose. It all the time ends up this way whenever
the subject comes up about ... (*Gestures to the shrine.*)
him. Come on inside here now before that sun roasts
you up alive.

MONA. (*Entering.*) If you think it's hot here, you
should really have been there in Marfa.

JUANITA. (*Fanning herself with a menu.*) Was
things there just like you was hopin' they'd be?

MONA. There's hardly anythin' left to Reata anymore. If nobody knew what was there, they'd never
know it was that beautiful house from "Giant," A
bunch of telephone poles stickin' up outta the ground
is all that's left standin' ... the rest is just lyin'
all over the ground rottin' away in the hot sun.
(SHE *goes to her suitcase.*) I managed to retrieve
one last identifiable piece of it ... one of those pieces
that, I believe, was along the top of the porch roof.
I had to really dig among those piles of destruction
to find one that even had the slightest hint of recogni-
tion. (SHE *produces a chunk of plaster with a hint
of architectural definition.*) Isn't it beautiful?

JUANITA. (*Glancing over it.*) Some of those you
got in past years are better.

MONA. (*Somewhat disappointed.*) You really think
so? (*Suddenly defensive.*) Souvenier hunters with
thoughts of financial profit have absconded with all
the really recognizable ones. Why, you know, that

house, for a time, was as much a landmark as the Empire State Building in New York City, New York. (*Fondling the piece of Reata.*) It was only the front, of course, that's the way they do things in the movies ... deceivin' to the eye, they call it. (SHE *sets the piece of Reata on the shrine.*) If I don't wash some of this dust and stickiness from my body, I will scream.

JUANITA. You need to soak in a nice cool tub an' relax.

MONA. A sink bath in the ladies' room will suffice me for the time bein'. I feel so guilty wastin' our precious water supply on bathin' more than twice a week. I will be so grateful when this horrible dry spell is over and water again flows instead of trickles into this town.

JUANITA. It can't last forever.

MONA. (*Near the back room door.*) It will be so embarrassin' to have the Disciples return to see how this town has dried-up so ... (*The thunder and rain slowly fade up and the lights start their fade to 1955.*) ridin' in on that bus it looked like a regular ghost town ...

MONA (THEN). (*Off.*) Juanita ...

MONA. Seems hard to believe how it has all changed so quickly. (*Looks around her.*) It hasn't changed much in here, though. They'll all remember how it was in here ... in the five-and-dime. (MONA *stands in a trance as* MONA (THEN) *enters past her from the back room.*)

MONA (THEN). Juanita, Sissy just told me about Joe. Why? ... Why did Sidney have to fire him?

JUANITA. My Sidney has done what he believes

is best for that boy, as well as the rest of us. You'll understand better as you get older.

MONA (THEN). What did he do that was so wrong? He never bothered nobody, just stocked the shelves an' oiled the floors like he was paid to.

JUANITA. It's nothin' to do with his work, it's what he is. Things'll be better without him around, Sidney has done the right thing.

MONA (THEN). But we're friends!

JUANITA. He should have friends who are boys, not you and Sissy. It's shameful the way you three dressed up as look-alikes an' pretended you were that singin' act ... What's their names?

MONA (THEN). The McGuire Sisters ... and that was just for the Senior Talent Show ... for fun, that's all ... just for fun.

JUANITA. Well, it didn't turn out that way. Everybody who saw it was shocked and disgusted. Then there was that incident at the final school dance with Lester T. Callahan, that has erupted into a regular scandal ... he is a sick boy that should be treated before he grows up into a communist.

MONA (THEN). No, Juanita, you're wrong ... you're all wrong. He's different from all them others, that's all.

JUANITA. Sidney knows what is best.

MONA (THEN). No, he doesn't.

JUANITA. Sidney an' me are good upstandin', Bible-believin' Christians ... an' we've searched our Bible from cover to cover to find an excuse for that boy's behavior an' there is none. In the eyes of God he doesn't belong.

MONA (THEN). If God doesn't accept him, then ... then I can't accept God, then.

JUANITA. (*Grabs her angrily.*) Listen here, young lady ... I will not permit you to speak of our Lord that way.

MONA (THEN. (*Pulling away.*) He's not my God. I don't want him ... I hate him! (*The lights begin to return to the* 70's.) I hate him ... and I hate Sidney, too. (SHE *rushes into the backroom.*)

JUANITA. (*Following her.*) You have a lot to learn, young lady, if you expect to live in this world.

MONA. It just makes me cry sometimes ... doesn't it you, Juanita? ... to remember how active this town was, before the rain stopped comin'

JUANITA. (*In the back room rummaging on a shelf.*) The Lord will send rain, when he's ready.

(*From outside,* SISSY *is heard calling "Juanita" from down the street.*)

MONA. (*Laughs.*) Well, I hope we'll all recognize what it is when it arrives.

(SISSY *enters hurridly carrying a bag of groceries and a newspaper.* SHE *is the same age as* MONA *with bleached hair pulled high atop her head. Her dress is flashy and extremely short.* SHE *wears as much dimestore jewelry as* SHE *can get away with. The single outstanding feature about* SISSY *is her gigantic breasts ... large to the point of being abnormal ... awesome.*)

SISSY (*Entering.*) Juanita ... Hey, Juanita, guess what? (*Seeing* MONA.) Hey, kid ... I see your bus finally managed to pull on in. Who was drivin' today, the cute Willie-Boy Brophy? Whew! ... He can punch my ticket any-ol' time he wants.

JUANITA. (*Entering from the back room.*) What are you so all-fired up about, Sissy?

SISSY. (*Flashes the newspaper at her.*) You two are never gonna guess what's in today's "Odessa-American!"

JUANITA. News of a rain storm comin'?

SISSY. (*Smugly.*) Nope ... the "Ice Capades."

JUANITA. The what?!

SISSY. The "Ice Capades"...They're comin' to the Ector County Coliseum for three whole days ... and that's not all. . (SHE *spreads the newspaper out over the table.*) Read ... read what it says here in this article ... They're goin' to hold tryouts to find new skaters to join up with 'em .. My God, when I read that, my heart skipped four beats. It's my big chance ... the chance of my lifetime!

JUANITA. (*Dumbly.*) To do what?

SISSY. What do you mean, to do what?... ice skate with 'em, that's what.

MONA. (*Laughing.*) You?

SISSY. Well, I ain't talkin' 'bout my Aunt Sally.

JUANITA. The only skatin' you know how to do is roller skatin', an' you ain't done none of that since the Dixie Roller Rink closed up nearly ten years ago.

SISSY. Skatin's, skatin'. I don't care if you do it on rollers, ice ... or water, for Chrissake. It's all just a matter of balance an' form ... an' God knows my form is well balanced. (SHE *throws out her chest to them.*)

MONA. Aren't you just a little late into life for somethin' like that?

SISSY. Late for you, maybe ... but I'm just beginnin'. Hell, you'd think from the way you two
are talkin' I was nearly over the hill, an' ready
for a wheelchair.

JUANITA. You'd be less apt to break your neck
wheelin' on ice, than skatin' on it.

(MONA *joins her in a laugh.*)

SISSY. You're gonna be laughin' outta the other
side of your mouth ... just wait an' see.

MONA. That sure is some fancy new dress you're
wearin' there, Sissy. Did you get it special for tonight?

SISSY. Mimi Gonzolez made it up for me from
a picture in a magazine. (*Models it.*) It's the cat's
ass, ain't it?

JUANITA. It's too short, an' mind your language.

SISSY. I gotta keep up with the times, don't I?

JUANITA. The "times" is havin' trouble keepin'
up with you, if you're askin' me.

SISSY. Well, I ain't.

MONA. It looks like one of them skatin' outfits
you used to wear all the time.

SISSY. (*Laughs.*) Ya, it kinda does, don't it ...
Hey, remember how they'd all scream an' yell when
I'd skate out onto that floor ... glidin' an' twirlin'
aroun' that roller rink like a ... what? ... what
was it they used to call me?

JUANITA. Scandalous ... that's what I called the
way you always showed off ... bouncin' yourself all
over the place.

SISSY. Well, as the good Lord says ... "if you got 'em ... bounce 'em. (SHE *discovers a stain on her dress*.) Godamn that Luke Dempsey and his oily hands ... Just look at the stain he left here on my dress ... dammit all to hell!

JUANITA. (*Unpacking the groceries*.) You keep that kinda talk for the truck-stop, not ... Sissy, you forgot the bread ... how can ya make sandwiches without ..

SISSY. Well, I got everythin' else didn't I! You got any stain remover aroun'?

JUANITA. (*Starts for the door*.) Out back.

SISSY. Out back, where?

JUANITA. Out back there on that shelf with the cleanin' stuff.

SISSY. Where you goin'?

JUANITA. To buy the bread you forgot. (SHE *exits*.)

SISSY. Jeezus, you'd think I'd commited a mortal sin or somethin' ... hell, it's only bread. (SHE *starts for the backroom*.)

MONA. (*Lost in memory*.) Joe used to call you "Swanya Henie, the breastest bird on eight wheels." (*Laughs and turns to* SISSY.) Remember?

SISSY. Joe?! ... Hell, I ain't thought about him in ages. What made you remember him all of a sudden? (SHE *exits out of sight into the back room.* MONA *follows, but not out of sight. The lights start to cross fade to* 1955.)

MONA. I don't know ... he just sort of popped into mind, that's all. I was doin' a lot a thinkin' back there in Marfa ... at Reata, and ... He's still in my head I guess. (SHE *sits on a crate losing herself again to the past*.)

SISSY. (*Off*.) The three of us really had ourselves

one helluva good time back then, didn't we'' That
Joe Qualley was a real riot, wasn't he?

(SISSY (THEN) *followed by* MONA *enter from the*
back room into the store. SHE *has the same*
gigantic boobs forcing her thin sweater to its
limit. SHE *also wears a short skating skirt.*
MONA (THEN) *is helping her carry boxes of*
cosmetics that they will hang from the display
rack.)

SISSY (THEN). (*Entering.*) Me an' Joe was gonna
get Stella May to take your place doin' the McGuire
Sisters, but she wouldn't have been as good as you.

MONA (THEN). I don't think we should do that
act anymore because of all that's happened. Juanita
says it was that thing at the senior dance with
Lester T. Callahan that started all the trouble.

SISSY (THEN). I thought it was a riot, a real
riot. They all thought he was my cousin from Oklahoma City . . . especially Lester T.

MONA (THEN). He really does make a very pretty
girl, doesn't he?

SISSY (THEN). Lester T. sure thought so, didn't
he? . . . thought he was the cutest thing he'd ever
seen. I would have given anythin' to see the expres-
sion on his face when he got Joe in the backseat
of his car, reached in his dress, squeezed them
balloons and strawberry jello exploded all over his
rented white tuxedo. (*Laughs.*) Serves the bastard
right for two-timin' me right in front of my face.

MONA (THEN). Joe should never have carried the
joke so far. You think Lester T. will ever get even
with him like he said?

SISSY (THEN). Shoot, I wouldn't put it past that goon-head.

MONA (THEN). It's been nearly three months. Maybe he's forgot.

SISSY (THEN). He ain't forgot ... hell, it's the only thing outta twelve years of school he's remembered. (*Looks out the window.*) Thank God, that rain's finally gonna stop. I got me a date over at the graveyard tonight.

MONA (THEN). We've got a meetin' of the "Disciples," did you forget?

SISSY (THEN). The meetin' ain't gonna last all night is it? I just can't get over your bein' back ... seems like I'm dreamin' or somethin'.

MONA (THEN). (*Excited.*) Oh, me too. (*They hug.*) I missed you so very much.

SISSY (THEN). And me, you.

MONA (THEN). I was so afraid for this summer to be over. Now it can stay summer forever, can't it?

SISSY (THEN). Shoot, I hope not. The heat's been so hot I think it's beginnin' to shrink my "bazooms." (*Throws out her chest.*) They look like they've shrunk any to you?

MONA (THEN). (*Inspecting.*) They both look the same to me.

SISSY (THEN). You think they might be as big as Marilyn Monroe's?

MONA (THEN). I think they might be bigger.

SISSY (THEN). (*Thrilled.*) You really mean it? Sidney said they were, but you know him.

MONA (THEN). He told you that?

SISSY (THEN). He's such a card...always pinchin' my bottom behin' one of the counters. Not where Juanita can see him though. She thinks he's as prim an' proper as a preacher. Boy, does he pull the wool over her eyes.

MONA (THEN). Where is he today, anyhow?... hung over again?

SISSY (THEN). Had some kinda meetin' over in Waco. (SHE *takes a lipstick, eyebrow pencil, etc. from the rack and applies them.*)

MONA (THEN). I'll never forgive him for firin' Joe.

SISSY (THEN). Well, whattaya expect from the buttholes in this town?

MONA (THEN). I'm afraid he might leave town now he's got no job.

SISSY (THEN). Hey, you got a thing for him maybe?

MONA (THEN). No!

SISSY (THEN). You do! That's why you really came back, ain't it?

MONA (THEN). (*Quickly.*) It was my asthma... my asthma...we're friends, that's all...just like you an' me.

SISSY. (THEN). O.K. . . . O.K. . . . Jeez, I was only kiddin'...Here try some of this new cheek blush that just come in. (*Starts to apply it on her.*) Hey, ain't you just bustin' for that movie to come out so's you can see yourself up there on the movie screen with James Dean? (*A squeal and a shiver.*) Ooh! He can drag me off to the graveyard any ol' night he wants...rainin' or not.

MONA (THEN). (*Nervous.*) Did you ever dream about what it would be like? You know, to make love to somebody real famous like him?

SISSY (THEN). All the time . . . but you really should experiment with some "nobody" before you tackle someone as important as him. That's all I'm doin' . . . sort of like homework for the big test later on. I just can't get over somebody your age haven' never been over to the graveyard with anyone before.

MONA (THEN). It's . . . it's too spooky.

SISSY (THEN). Oh, you get used to it after awhile. Some of the guys get scared an' have trouble gettin' goin', but they're mainly after my "bazooms" anyhow. They all gotta squeeze an' feel aroun' . . . most of 'em get their kicks just doin' that.

MONA (THEN). Aren't you afraid you'll get caught?

SISSY (THEN). Shoot, nobody goes over to that ol' graveyard no more. It's all grown over with stickers an' tall grass, an' the gravestones have all been pushed over to use for layin' places. I always do it on top of Colonel Jaspar P. Ramslan' the second . . . soun's dreamy, don't he?

MONA (THEN). Wouldn't it be terrible to be left alone like that with nobody to pick the weeds off your body.

SISSY (THEN). Mona, how creepy!

MONA (THEN). I don't know anybody's who's ever died, an' I hope I never do. I'm so afraid I might never remember them anymore.

SISSY (THEN). (*Laughs.*) What the hell's that supposed to mean?

MONA (THEN). (*Laughs also.*) I don't know. I'm always sayin' stuff like that I can't explain.

SISSY (THEN). I can get in enough trouble sayin' stuff I *can* explain. (*Gets moving.*) I better get the rest of them boxes unpacked before Juanita gets back ... c'mon an' help me.

MONA (THEN). Sissy, I feel somethin' so deep inside me about James Dean that I can't get words to come out about it.

SISSY (THEN). You mean love?

MONA (THEN). No, it's somethin' more.

SISSY (THEN). More than love? There's nothin' more than love ... love's the end.

MONA (THEN). No, Sissy, you're wrong. There's somethin' beyond the end. (*The lights start to cross-fade*) As soon as I can save up enough money, I'm gonna buy Reata ... an' you an' me an' Joe will move there an' live forever an' ever ... Wouldn't that be wonderful.

SISSY (THEN). But it's only the front, silly ... it's not a real house .. c'mon. (SHE *exits* MONA (THEN) *rushes after her*)

MONA (THEN). It could be, Sissy ...

MONA. (*To herself.*) It's just "deceivin' to the eye," that's all.

(SISSY *enters from the back, wiping her dress.*)

SISSY. What is?

MONA. (*Shaken from her memory.*) What? ... Oh, nothin'.

SISSY. That oil stain look like it's gone to you?

MONA. I can't see it from here.

(JUANITA *enters with a loaf of bread.* SISSY *and* MONA *come out of the backroom.*)

JUANITA. Mona, you gonna go freshen yourself up, or ain't ya? . . . It's gettin' awful late.

MONA. (*Looks at her watch.*) My, I just seem to have lost all track of time. (*Gets her suitcase and goes into the backroom.*) I'll be right back.

SISSY. (*To* JUANITA.) Somethin' eatin' at her, or what? . . She's actin' awful strange.

JUANITA. That long, hot bus ride turned her all inside-out, I guess. (*Starts to make sandwiches.*) You ain't serious about his Ice Capades business, are ya?

SISSY. Hell, if I ain't. (*Gets nail polish from the display rack.*)

JUANITA. You'd just be makin' a fool of yourself, an' you know it.

SISSY. (*Setting at a table and putting polish on her nails.*) Well, it's my life to fool aroun' with, ain't it?

JUANITA. I'm gonna ask my Wednesday night prayer club to devote our next few sessions to you.

SISSY. Better pray for them poor people over in China, they need it a helluva lot more than me.

JUANITA. We stopped prayin' for them. It didn't seem to be doin' much good. We're now prayin' for rain.

SISSY. I doubt you'll do any better than ya did for them poor Chinese . . . which is why I prefer you don't go prayin' for me. Frankly, I've found prayin' to be more of a curse.

JUANITA. Sissy!

SISSY. Oh, I used to pray . . . prayed all the time when I needed help. Never did a whole helluva lot of good though. Then, when I stopped ... hell, everythin' started in to happen. So, you've prob'bly done them Chinese a great big favor.

MONA. (*Entering.*) I turned on both them faucets an' nothin' comes out.

SISSY. Well, it's finally happened.

JUANITA. (*Sharply.*) *Nothin's* happened! (*To* MONA.) Did you turn 'em all the way?

MONA. As far as they'll go.

SISSY. You can't turn 'em no further than that. (SHE *goes to the door, waving her arms to dry her nails.*)

JUANITA. The pressure in the pipes must be down ... wait a while an' try again.

SISSY. Pressure, hell ... the water's all gone for Chrissakes.

MONA. Three years without the benefit of rain. That must be some kinda record for a dry-spell, don't ya think?

SISSY. Everythin's just dryin' up an' dyin' away all aroun' us.

JUANITA. It will rain again soon I have faith in prayer, an' the Lord.

SISSY. (*At the door.*) Look at this thermometer for Chrissake ... ninety-nine degrees. Can you believe it?! Hey, Juanita, how hot does that Bible of yours say it gets in hell?

JUANITA. The Holy Bible does not deal in that sort of information.

SISSY. Well, I'm willin' to bet it's cooler there, than it is here, by ten degrees or more ... Yes sir, them Ice Capades are comin' to rescue my ass, just in time.

MONA. Sissy, did Luke say anythin' about that old fan?

SISSY. Said he'd come take a look at it first minute he had.

MONA. You think maybe it's just stuck?

SISSY. Juanita, hand me that broom over there an' we'll just find out.

JUANITA. (*Getting broom.*) What are you gonna do?

SISSY. Bang on them blades an' see if I can unstick it.

JUANITA. Careful you don't break it.

SISSY. How the hell can I break it if it's already broken.

JUANITA. Well, you could bend one of the blades, or . . .

SISSY. Hush up an' foot yourself on over there an' flick that switch back an' forth.

JUANITA. (*Goes to the switch.*) What good will that do?

SISSY. How the hell do I know? . . . Maybe it's just been "off" all this time . . . you flickin' (SHE *bangs on the blades with the broom handle.*)

JUANITA. Yes. (SHE *flicks the switch back and forth.*) Nothin's happenin'.

SISSY. (*Stops.*) No shit, Dick Tracy. (*Moves away disgustedly.*) How the hell they expect people to come in this rat-hole an' buy up their nickle an' dime crap in this heat, is beyond me.

JUANITA. It's just Mexicans anymore an' they're used to it.

SISSY. Even a goddam wetback has a right to be cool.

MONA. Maybe it's better the fan stays broken. It would only stir up lots of dust an' dead air, anyhow.

SISSY. If everybody don't hurry up an' get themselves here, all they'll find is our bleached bones. (*To* MONA) Hey, you ain't even said how you like the decorations . . . took me off a whole days work from the truck stop to get 'em strung up.

MONA. I think they're just perfect.

SISSY. (*Noticing a dangling streamer.*) Aw crap, that one's fell down already. (SHE *goes to the ladder.*) Hand me that end, would ya, honey? (MONA *hands it to her as* SHE *climbs the ladder.*) My God, the higher I climb, the hotter it gets. (*Laughter.*) Wouldn't it just tick everybody off though, if all their lives they worked their butts off to get to heaven an' hell turned out to be the coolest spot all along?

MONA. (*Goes to the door.*) Where on earth is Jimmy Dean? I hope nothin's happened to him.

SISSY. Oh . . . He's workin'.

MONA. Workin'?! . . . What do you mean, workin' . . . Where?

SISSY. For Luke . . . over at the Texaco, puttin' patches on innertubes.

MONA. Doin' what?!

SISSY. Patchin' holes on innertubes. Luke's givin' him fifty cents a hole.

MONA. (*Upset.*) Luke's just takin' advantage of that boy's mental deficiency. I don't like that. I don't like that one bit!

SISSY. Oh, for Chrissake, Mona! He's havin' hisself a good time . . . leave him alone.

MONA. Luke's just tryin' to make a laughin' stock of him infront of the whole town.

SISSY. Nobody's laughin', Goddammit.

MONA. (*Frantic.*) They are! They laugh all the time . . . to themselves.

SISSY. Oh, Mona, you just *think* they do.

MONA. I *know* they do, because they're jealous . . . jealous because I was the one chosen to bring the son of Jimmy Dean into this world. (*Goes to the door.*) I am surprised at both of you for allowin' Luke to take advantage of . . . (SHE *goes outside and calls.*) Jimmy Dean! . . . Jimmy Dean!

SISSY. Mona, for Chrissake, he's old enough to . . .

MONA. (*Storms back in. Sharply at* SISSY.' This is none of your business!

JUANITA. (*To* MONA.) Calm yourself down now, or you'll get your asthma to . . .

MONA. (*To* SISSY.) You sound just like them . . . (*Gestures to the door.*) out there . . . those warped an' demented people who think they know so much more than all them doctors I have spent every penny I have earned workin' here in this dimestore, to take him to. He is retarded in the brain . . . a moron!

SISSY. Don't you call him no moron, dammit!

MONA. I will call him what he is. Oh, those doctors have their fancy names to confuse you . . . but the truth is . . . he's a moron! (SHE *starts to wheeze and gasp for breath.*) Mentally equal to a child between . . . the ages . . . the ages of . . . of eight and . . . (SHE *grabs a chair for support.* JUANITA *rushes to her.*)

JUANITA. Now see what you've gone an' done. Where's your pills?

(MONA *gestures to her purse.* JUANITA *gets them along with the remainder of her Orange Crush.*)

SISSY. It may not be none of my business, but it is just as warped an' demented to keep him cooped up in here all day, 'cause you're afraid of them laughin' at *you* ... not him, Mona ... but you!

JUANITA. Sissy, you stay out of this, Jimmy Dean is her son, not yours.

SISSY. I thought he belonged to James Dean fans everywhere ... conceived in Mona, an' dedicated to the population.

MONA. He chose me from everyone else to bring his child into this world.

SISSY. Three cheers for Mona Magadalene!

MONA. (*Moving to* SISSY *on the ladder.*) You are a vile, jealous an' wicked person ... just like all the others in this town! (SHE *grabs the ladder and frantically tries to shake her off.* JUANITA *tries to pull* MONA *away.*)

JUANITA. Mona! ... Mona, stop ... you'll make her fall.

SISSY. (*Escaping down the ladder.*) Mona, for Chrissake, you gone crazy or somethin'?

MONA (*Moving away.*) I don't know why you have turned against me ... my friend, the only friend I ...

SISSY. All I said was ..

MONA. I heard what you had to say, that he should be locked up in one of them institutions for crazy people ... the same kinda remarks "they" have been sayin' behind my back ever since I discovered the truth about him!

SISSY. I never said any ... !

MONA. They're not goin' to take Jimmy Dean away from me, you hear?! ... an' neither are you. You have turned out to be just as warped an' demented as they are.

SISSY. You were born an' raised in this town too, Miss!

MONA. Yes ... but I rose above the attitudes of this town while you layed spread over a gravestone an' took them inside you.

JUANITA. Mona!

(SISSY *stunned to silence, stares at* MONA *in disbelief.* MONA *nervously moves away. The sound of a passing train is heard in the distance.*)

MONA. Juanita, would you call the Texaco for me an' have Luke send Jimmy Dean back, right away.

SISSY. You have gone one step too far this time, Mona. (SISSY *goes to the door.*)

JUANITA. Sissy, where you goin?

SISSY. Outside to cool off. Ain't that a joke, though! (SHE *exits.*)

JUANITA. (*Going to the phone.*) Mona, that was a terrible thing to say to her.

MONA (THEN). (*Dreamily to herself in the back room.*) I dream about it all the time ... me an' James Dean all tangled up in each other's arms under the stars ... All peaceful an' quiet with only the slightest summer breeze.

(*The shadow of* JOE *again appears behind the screen door. His face is bruised and bleeding.* MONA *catches sight of him out of the corner of her eye before* HE *quickly disappears.*)

MONA. Jimmy Dean?

JUANITA. Where?

MONA. Out of the corner of my eye ... I thought I saw ... someone.

MONA (THEN). (*To* SISSY (THEN) *who has joined* MONA (THEN) *in the back room.* This has been the most wonderful summer of my whole entire life ... an' it's goin' away. I'm scared, Sissy, I can't let it go. Everythin's been so different since bein' in "Giant," an' meetin' James Dean.

SISSY (THEN). What's to be scared of, silly? ... Hey, you got yourself into some kinda trouble you ain't tellin' me about?

MONA (THEN). (*Moving quickly away.*) I can't tell you ... I can't.

(SISSY *follows after her.*)

MONA. (*To herself.*) It should have been the beginnin' of the summer that night, instead of the end.

JUANITA. (*Into the phone.*) Hello, Luke ... Juanita, Is Jimmy Dean still over there with you? ... He did? How long ago was that? ... I see ... I see ...

Thank you Luke. See you at the prayer club Wednesday night. (SHE *hangs up.*) Luke says he rushed on over to the railroad sidin' to count box-cars on that passin' freight ... Sounds like a long one. He counted eighty-five on Saturday. Maybe today he'll count a hundred ... that's his goal.

MONA (*Still in a dreamlike trance.*) He's all I have left to remind me. I don't know how I could ever face tomorrow, or the day after, or the day after that without the memory he brings to mind for me so strongly. (*Wiping her forehead and snapping out of her trance.*) My, that long weekend in Marfa has left me so ... so nostalgic or somethin'. (*Again,* SHE *catches sight of* JOE *peering through the screen door.* SHE *rushes to the door.*) Boy!

JUANITA. What boy? (HE *disappears.*)

MONA. At the door ... the same one I thought I saw before.

JUANITA. Who was he?

MONA. (*Puzzled.*) I don't know. He was there, an' he just disappeared. (*Sees something outside.*) Juanita, come here, quick.

JUANITA. Now what's the matter? (*Joins her at the door.*)

MONA. Someone's arrivin' in one of them little sports cars ... see ... there, across the street.

JUANITA. Is it Stella May?

MONA. I don't think so ... Whoever it is, they're alone.

JUANITA. Can you see who it is, then?

MONA. I can't tell ... it's a lady though, an' she's lookin' over here at the store.

JUANITA. You think it could be one of them Disciples?... Martha Gibbons, or ... Sue Ellen?

MONA. I certainly hope not ... I haven't changed or nothin' (*Moves from the door quickly.*) Oh, oh ... She's comin' right this way ... Juanita, move away ... She's gonna know we've been gapin' at her.

(*It's too late.* JOANNE *enters.* SHE *is a very classy in a lightweight pants suit.* SHE *wears large sunglasses.*)

JUANITA. Hello.

JOANNE. Hello.

JUANITA. We was just lookin' at that funny lookin' car you're drivin'.

MONA. It's a sports car, Juanita.

JUANITA. I know. I know ... still funny lookin' to me ... don't know how you can squeeze yourself all up inside it. (*Laughs.*) Must make you feel like a sardine in a can.

JOANNE. (*Giving her a half smile.*) Don't see many dime stores like this around anymore.

JUANITA. Still a few of us left hangin' on. Is there somethin' I can help you to find?

JOANNE. (*Caught off guard.*) Umm ... (*Removes her sunglasses.*) Sunglasses ... One of the lenses on these is cracked, and it's become very irritating to look through.

JUANITA. There's a few pair left hangin' on the wall over there. (*Gestures to a spot near the shrine.*)

JOANNE. Thank you. (SHE *goes to it.*)

MONA. Are you just passin' through?

JOANNE. You might say.

MONA. Not many people do, anymore ... what with the super highway ignorin' us the way it did.

JOANNE. (*Looking up at the photos of Dean.*) I used to be a fan of his, too.

MONA. Not anymore?

JOANNE. (*Bluntly.*) He died ... didn't you know?

MONA. Well, of course, I know ... but he lives on in his movies and ... did you happen to see "Giant?" It was filmed not far from here, in Marfa. I don't mean to sound boastful, but I was in that picture. Only in the crowd scenes, but my face does appear on the screen distinctly in one segment.

JOANNE. That must have been very exciting for you.

MONA. It was *the* most exciting time of my whole entire life. (*Curious.*) Your voice ... it sounds so very familiar.

JOANNE. (*Going to the counter and mirror with several pair of glasses to check out how they look.*) People have said it's unusual. I've heard it all my life so it sounds perfectly normal to me.

MONA. (*Laughs.*) Well, yes ... I suppose it would.

JOANNE. Are you the mother of his son? (*Gestures back to the photos.*)

MONA. (*Feigned surprise.*) How on earth did you know about that?

JOANNE. I saw one of your signs down by the highway ... "See the son of James Dean, visit Kressmont's five-and-dime, nine miles ahead."

MONA. (*Embarrassed laugh.*) We never bothered to take them down because the words became so faded from the sun they couldn't be read anymore.

JOANNE. (*To* JUANITA.) I believe I'll take these.

(*Removes money from her purse.*)

JUANITA. Will there be anythin' else?

JOANNE. Yes, could I have a glass of water?

JUANITA. (*Embarrassed.*) We seem to be temporarily out of water. Would you settle for an Orange Crush instead?

JOANNE. As long as it's cold and wet.

MONA. When little Jimmy Dean was first born, nearly three thousand people swarmed into town over a one week period, just to see the son of James Dean. He really put McCarthy, Texas on the roadmap for a brief, but glorious period of time. We were the busiest most prosperous Kressmont store in all of Texas.

JUANITA. They gave us a plaque...see it on the wall over there.

MONA. Juanita's husband, Sidney, was the manager at the time. He has passed away since.

JOANNE. And were the signs *his* idea?

MON. Why yes...he had the whole thing planned out perfect. There were newspaper an' magazine people here takin' pictures an' writin' down everythin' I would say...I was quite a celebrity. People bought up everythin' they could get their hands on thinkin' little Jimmy Dean had touched it. He was on display on a platform over there by the window. Sidney had to hire two policemen just to protect him from possible molesters an' kidnappers. It wasn't only the five-an'-dime neither...the entire town went through a period of immense prosperity.

JUANITA. They even elected Sidney mayor after that.

MONA. You really should have seen this town before ... it really was quite active for one its size, but now most everybody has been drawn away to greener an' *damper* pastures. (*A small laughter.*)

JOANNE. And you?

MONA. (*Surprised at the question.*) Me? ... Why, I'm quite content to remain where I am.

JOANNE. There's not much chance of any growth here in all this dust, is there?

MONA. (*Amused.*) That seems to be rather an extremely personal question comin' from a stranger. (SHE *is becoming very nervous.*) Juanita, do you think that water pressure has risen enough by now? (SHE *turns to see* JOE *again outside the door.*) There he is again! (HE *runs off.*)

JUANITA. I didn't see anyone.

MONA. It looked like he was hurt an' bleedin'... an' he wanted to come in.

JUANITA. You sure it wasn't just Jimmy Dean?

MONA. Hurt an' bleedin? (*Goes out the door.*) Jimmy Dean, you out there?!

(SISSY *approaches her outside.*)

SISSY. Mona ... Mona, I wanna talk to you about ...

MONA. I don't wanna talk to you. (SHE *re-enters the store.*) Juanita, you don't suppose somethin's happened to him. (*A car horn is heard blaring down the street.*)

SISSY. (*Outside.*) Here comes Stella an' Edna Louise!

JOANNE. (*Nervously wanting an escape. To* JUA-NITA.) Excuse me, could I use your ladies room?

JUANITA. Right through them curtains there, an' straight ahead. (JOANNE *exits.* MONA *is drawn to her momentarily.*)

STELLA. (*Outside.*) Sissy!... Sissy, honey is that you?

SISSY. (*To* STELLA.) It ain't my Aunt Sally.. Park that thing you're drivin' an' come on in. (SHE *enters the store.*) Shit, would you get a look at the size of that car she's drivin'!

JUANITA. (*To* SISSY.) You've been drinkin', haven't you?

SISSY. Drinkin' what?

JUANITA. Alcohol. I can smell it on your breath.

SISSY. There ain't no water. I had to drink me somethin' or die of thirst.

(STELLA MAY *and* EDNA LOUISE *appear at the door. There is much squeeling and yelling as they all converge on each other with hugs and kisses.* STELLA *is the same age as the others.* EDNA *is several years younger.* STELLA *is loud, boisterous and obnoxious, a small town girl who married into money* SHE *wasn't prepared for.* SHE *is dressed to the hilt in the best of everything, and then some. Over her dress,* SHE *now wears a red windbreaker. Across the back in script is written, "Disciples of James Dean."* EDNA LOUISE *is plain and simple.* SHE *wears a white stained beautician's uniform which is pulled tight across her obviously pregnant front. Her stringy hair is pulled back into an attempted ponytail.*

SHE *wears beat-up saddle shoes and white anklets and carries a clear plastic cleaning bag which contains a party dress.*)

SISSY. (*As they enter.*) Stella May, you old shit-kicker, how the hell are you?

EDNA. I didn't have time to change after work cause Stella May was in such a hurry to get here ... I feel so embarrassed.

SISSY. Edna, you got somethin' cookin' there in your oven?

EDNA. (*Dumbly.*) I beg your pardon? (SHE *suddenly realizes the joke and holds her pregnancy.*) Oh! (*Giggles.*) Yes ... my seventh.

STELLA. Seven kids! Can you imagine anythin' more horrible! (SHE *models the jacket.*) Hey! ... Hey, everybody, look what I found up in my attic. (SHE *laughs* ... SHE *always laughs.*) Ain't it a hoot?!

MONA. The old club jacket.

EDNA. (*Frantically trying to pull hers out of her bag.*) I have mine too ... it seems to be stuck here in my bag, but ... I do have it!

SISSY. Jeezus, can you believe we used to wear them things?

STELLA. Sissy, my God it's so good to see you ... Last I heard of you was a Christmas card from Oklahoma City 'bout five years ago.

SISSY. Lived there ten years ... I'm back here now, goin' on three ... been workin' ever at the "Flyin' 'H' Truck Stop" down by the highway. Got me plans for movin' on though ... real soon.

STELLA. From the looks of things out there, you'd better start movin' on quick. Christ, what's happened

to this town, anyway? I've seen dead dogs layin'
out 'long the side of the road with more life than
this town's got.

JUANITA. Lack of rain's just about dried us all
up.

EDNA. (*To* JUANITA.) I will have to use your
bathroom to change. (SHE *wanders around the store,
looking.*)

STELLA. Mona, you ain't changed a day ... hell,
none of you has. (*Laughs.*) Hey, what about me?
(*Twirls around.*) Think I've changed, huh?

SISSY. Honey, you look like a million bucks.

STELLA. Million an' a half. (*Laughs.*) My Merle just
brought him in another one. That man can smell oil,
I swear.

EDNA. (*Who has put a penny in the gum-ball machine and holds up the gum-ball.*) Look! ... Look,
everybody ... Red, my favorite color. My fortune
in the newspaper said today would be my lucky
day ... (*Pops it in her mouth.*) an' it is.

STELLA. Ain't she a dip though? (*Looks around.*)
Anybody else show up yet? (JOANNE *enters through
the curtains.* STELLA *sees her.*) Don't tell me now,
let me guess.

MONA. Stella, that's not ...

STELLA. No! ... no, let me guess. (*Quickly.*) Alice
Ann Johnson!

MONA. Stella, she's not ...

STELLA. I said don't tell me, for Chrissake! (SHE
sees the group picture on the table.) Oh, my God ...
the old group photograph ... aw! (*Goes to* SISSY
with it) My God, tell me that's not me.

SISSY. It ain't ... (*Points to opposite side.*) You're

over there with your tongue stickin' out. (EDNA *rushes over to look.*)

STELLA. My God, would ya get a look at that outfit I'm wearin'? (*Laughs.*) If any of the girls at the country club got their hands on this, I'd be black-balled.

EDNA. I have a party dress here in the bag. I haven't worn it in so long it smelled like moth balls, so I sent it to the dry cleaners, which is why it's . . .

STELLA. Oh Edna, quit belly achin' about the way you look. She's been harpin' about that damn dress all the damn day. Go put it on an' shut up. (*To* JOANNE.) As if it would make any difference.

JUANITA. The bathroom's right where it always was, Edna.

EDNA. I won't take very long, I promise. (SHE *exits.*)

SISSY. (*Calling after her.*) Don't flush the toilet whatever you do. It's the only water left in this whole damn town.

STELLA. (*Looking at* JOANNE *and then the picture.*) I just love to try an' guess at people from old photographs.

SISSY. (*Quietly to* JUANITA.) Who the hell is she?

JUANITA. Just someone passin' through.

STELLA. Hey Mona, is that fancy yellow sports car parked out front one of the purchases you made with all that money you raked in off Jimmy Dean?

MONA. There was no charge to see Jimmy Dean.

STELLA. There wasn't? You sure did miss out on a golden opportunity to cash in on a craze. (*To* JOANNE.) Then, it's gotta be yours then . . . You look like you've done pretty good for yourself.

JOANNE. I managed to do all right. (*A glance to* MONA.)

STELLA. You sure you're in this picture?

MONA. (*Very unnerved by* JOANNE's *continuous stares; quietly to* SISSY.) Did you see Jimmy Dean out there anywhere?

SISSY. Nope.

MONA. (*Goes to the door.*) Then where is he?... He couldn't have just disappeared into nowhere. (SHE *starts to wheeze and gasp for breath.*) ...Some... some...thing's...ha...happened...I...I can't catch my breath. (SHE *grabs onto the door frame for support.*)

STELLA. Get her some ice water. She's gonna faint for Chrissake.

SISSY. There ain't no water. (JUANITA *helps* MONA *to a seat.*)

JOANNE. Give her a swallow of whiskey.

JUANITA. There is no alcohol in this store an' there never will be.

JOANNE. What about that bottle Sidney used to keep hidden under the hardware counter?

JUANITA. (*Stunned.*) What do you...?

STELLA. (*Quickly.*) Martha Jane Gibbons!

JUANITA. Sidney did not drink!

JOANNE. Then how did he die from it?

SISSY. Who the hell are you?

JOANNE. He died from a decayed liver...he was eaten-up by alcohol.

SISSY. You can't go talkin' like that to her.

JUANITA. Sidney was a saint and he's in heaven now with God.

JOANNE. The only time he was ever in heaven is when he had a bottle in his hand.

JUANITA. Lies! . . . All lies!

(JOE *appears at the screen door.*)

MONA. (*Seeing* JOE *at the door in her memory.*) I think I know! . . . I think I know.

(SISSY (THEN) *enters from the back room with magazines for the rack.*)

STELLA. Christ, I named everybody in the picture it could be.

JOANNE. I'd find him collapsed in a corner, hiding from you and God . . . every Wednesday night when I came to put another layer of oil on the floor.

(MONA (THEN) *comes through the curtain.*)

JOE. (*Opening the door.*) MONA!

MONA. Oh my God . . . it's Joe!

MONA (THEN). (*Rushing to him at the door.*) Joe! . . . Sissy, it's Joe an' he's hurt an' bleedin'.

SISSY. Holy shit! . . . The McGuire Sisters are re-united!

(*The lights black and quickly.*)

ACT II

(The action is continuous.)

JOANNE. Surprise!

MONA (THEN). Sissy, get a wet cloth...quick!

JOE. Mona, what are you doin' back here?

MONA (THEN). Ssh!... You're mouth will bleed
some more.

MONA. *(Shocked.)* Joe!

JUANITA. (THEN). Get him out of this store...
get him out before somebody sees him!

STELLA. What the hell's goin' on?... I feel like
I'm standin' outside of an inside joke.

MONA (THEN). *(To* JUANITA.) He's hurt...can't
you see he's hurt bad?

JUANITA. (THEN). Then take him out back, out
of sight. *(Turns sharply to* JOANNE. You don't
know nothin'... Sidney was a saint.

*(MONA (THEN) and SISSY (THEN) take JOE to
the back room area.)*

SISSY. *(Going to* JOANNE *with open arms.)* Joe,
I can't believe it. Hell, you look better'n I do, for
Chrissake.

STELLA. *(Still studying the picture.)* Joe?! None

of the girls in this here picture was named ... (*Shock realization.*) Oh, my God!

(MONA (THEN) *is wiping blood from* JOE's *face.*)

SISSY (THEN). Did Lester T. do this to you?

JOE. He kept punchin' me in the face, while a couple of them others held me down, screamin' somethin' about how no pansy was goin' to make a jackass out of him ... then he ... he ...

STELLA. God, he looks just like a real girl, don't he?

SISSY (THEN). What, Joe? ...What?

JOE. They laid me face down over one of the gravestones, pulled down my overalls, an' Lester T. ... he ... oh, Mona, it was horrible ...

MONA. Joe, why did you have to come back here ... like this?

JOANNE. I had as much right to return for this reunion as anybody ... (*To everyone.*) didn't I?

SISSY (THEN). You're kiddin'! Lester T. did *that* to you?

JOE. He kept callin' me Joanne and ...

JUANITA. That's disgustin'!

SISSY (THEN). You'd better go see a doctor.

JOE. No!

MONA. I knew there was somethin' familiar about you ... I hope you enjoyed your little deception.

JOANNE. I never deceived you, Mona.

SISSY. Come on now, Joe, tell Mona you're sorry an' take off that wig an' stuff so's we can see how you *really* turned out.

STELLA. I didn't drive all the way from Amarillo

just to play "Who's a girl an' who ain't."

SISSY. Hey, remember... (*Starts to sing.*) "Sincerely ... on, yes ... Sincerely ..."

JUANITA. Those awful things you said about my Sidney were lies ... tell everybody they were all lies.

SISSY. Joe, Sidney's dead ... forget it, huh?

JOANNE. I thought this night was dedicated to remembering those days that made us all what we are today.

STELLA. Only the good times. I only wanna remember the good times.

SISSY. Hell, me too.

JUANITA. Sidney was a good man ... he was ...

JOANNE. He was a rotten son-of-a-bitch ... standing off there to the side of the graveyard fence ...

JOE. I saw faces. I know who they are.

JUANITA. Sidney was in Waco that day ... He wasn't even around.

JOANNE. (*Sharply to her.*) His *face* was there!

SISSY (THEN). How many of 'em were there?

JOE. Lester T. an' three of them others who always hang aroun' together ... but the whole town was there ... I saw 'em in my mind lined up there along the graveyard fence, yellin' an' cheerin' like a bunch of Mexicans at a cockfight ... Lester T. was just doin' the job this whole town's been wantin' to do to me for years.

MONA (THEN). Oh, Joe ... that's not true.

JOE. It *is* true. (*Holds his stomach.*) My God, I'm gonna be sick. (HE *rushes off.*)

SISSY (THEN). That Goddammed Lester T.! ... I'll cut off his wanger next time I get a hand on it. (SHE *exits*.)

MONA (THEN). Sissy, I don't want you to even see him no more... (SHE *follows* SISSY (THEN) *off*.) ... do you hear?

SISSY. O.K. You got all your revenge out now... let's get on with the party. It's hotter'n hell an' I'm dyin' for a cold beer.

JUANITA. Where do you have beer?

SISSY. Luke's keepin' a case cold for me in his soda-pop cooler.

JUANITA. You're not bringin' beer in here.

SISSY. Ah, come on Juanita... turn off God for tonight an' have a good time, huh?

JUANITA. I won't have a good time so long as he's in here.

JOANNE. *She*!

JUANITA. You are not a *she* . . . you're only pretendin' to be one like you always did.

JOANNE. (*Goes toward her, breasts high*.) Feel, go on and give them a good squeeze... there's no strawberry jello in these boobs.

MONA. Stop it... it was funny back then, but...

SISSY. (*Laughs*.) Aw, Mona, he's just pullin' her leg. (*Her laugh turns to surprise as* JOANNE *doesn't respond*.) ... aren't ya Joe?

JOANNE. I'm no longer Joe ... I'm Joanne.

SISSY. Joanne?!

MONA. What do you mean?

JOANNE. I mean unlike all of you ... I've undergone a change.

SISSY. A change?! What the hell are you talkin' about?

JOANNE. I don't have to pretend any more.

SISSY. You mean this is all ... real?!

STELLA. (*Shocked.*) Holy shit!

MONA. No ... No, I don't believe you.

SISSY. (*Stunned.*) Good God, Maude ... the wonders of modern science.

MONA. (*Moving away.*) That is disgustin'.

STELLA. (*Studying her.*) I've seen things like you on the T.V.... but I never saw one before, up close (*To everyone.*) any of you?

JUANITA. You're just one of them "perverts" ... that's what you are! (SHE *goes outside.* MONA *retreats to the shrine. The lights fade on the store and brighten in the backroom on* MONA (THEN) *and* JOE.)

JOE. I can't take any more crap from this town, Mona.

MONA (THEN). They're stupid. You have to remember that.

JOE. Run away with me, Mona ... The two of us could go away and ...

MONA (THEN). I can't leave, Joe ... I just got back ... the climate here is perfect for my asthma, the doctors said so. I might die if I ever leave again ...

JOE. Please, Mona ... we'll find another place ... It could be just like it was in Marfa, forever.

MONA (THEN). (*Disturbed.*) What happened in Marfa was ... we promised not to talk about that, remember?

JOE. You don't know how much I've missed you, Mona.

MONA (THEN). (*Nervous.*) I missed you, too, Joe ... an' Sissy, an' ...

JOE. You bein' away made me realize how much

I care for you, Mona ... how much I ... love you.

MONA (THEN.) Love! ... no, you only *think* you ...

JOE. No, it's real ... I know it's real ... love me back, Mona ... please?!

MONA (THEN). I can't do that, Joe ... not now.

JOE. One day? ... Do you think you will, one day?

MONA (THEN). One day ... maybe, but . .

JOE. We could get married, eventually ... that would show them I'm not the freak they think I am, wouldn't it? Mona, that night in Marfa was the happiest time of my life. (*Takes her hand.*)

MONA (THEN). (*Nervously pulls her hand away.*) I don't want to talk about it, Joe.

JOE. I actually *felt* like James Dean, there on the porch of ...

MONA (THEN). (*Angry.*) Joe, stop it! Maybe ... maybe you should go away ... just for awhile, until they all forget what's happened ... You could go visit your cousin in Tucson ... then, in a couple of months you could come back and ... and, maybe then ...

JOE. Would you marry me, then?

MONA (THEN). I don't know ... I need time to think about everythin' ... this summer has been so ... so, confusing

JOE. I need you, Mona ... I need you to help me decide just what the hell I am.

MONA. (THEN). Everythin's come about so sudden ... so, unexpected (*Starts to move away.*) I don't know what's gonna happen, now. (SHE *rushes out of the store.* SISSY (THEN) *enters the backroom as it slowly fades and the store brightens.*)

SISSY (THEN). Where's she runnin' off to?

JOE. (HE *turns and hugs* SISSY (THEN) *desperately.*) Oh, Sissy!

SISSY. I just can't get over it. Time sure does play crazy tricks, don't it?

SISSY (THEN). C'mon, I got some beer hidden out back . . . looks like you could use one. (THEY *exit.*)

SISSY. When'd this change-over of yours take place anyhow?

JOANNE. Thirteen years come January. Mama died from whatever it was she died from, and left a bundle in insurance money . . . and with it I became what Mama wanted all along . . . ironic, don't you think?

STELLA. I saw me a morphodite on a travellin' carnival once. They said it was a half-man, half-woman. Is that what you are? . . . in case anybody I know should ever ask.

JOANNE. Honey, you just tell 'em I'm a freak. All your friends should know what that is.

SISSY. C'mon, Stel, let's go get the beer. I need me one now more'n ever. (THEY *start to exit.*)

MONA. If you see Jimmy Dean out there, you drag him on back with you, you hear.

(EDNA LOUISE *enters wearing her party dress which is entirely too tight across her middle.* SHE *also wears high heels* SHE *can barely stand up in.*)

EDNA. Is everybody leavin' already?

STELLA. Good God, get a look at her, would ya? (*Laughs.*)

JUANITA. (*Entering from outside.*) Edna Louise

... my, don't you look nice, all fancied-up so.

EDNA. Thank you. This dress must have shrunk since the last time I got to wear it. The dry cleaners do that sometimes, I heard. (*Twirls.*) Do I look all right, otherwise?

MONA. Like a whole new person. How do you feel?

EDNA. (*Squirms.*) A little funny, I must admit. It seems awful tight an' isn't very comfortable, but I guess it's just 'cause I'm not used to dressin' up fancy like Stella May does all the time... Heavens if I don't sit down, I know I'll just fall off these stilts I'm wearin' an' break my neck. (SHE *wobbles to a chair.*)

STELLA. Honey, I think you look ridiculous.

EDNA. I do?

MONA. Stella, don't you have anythin' nice to say about anyone?

EDNA. Oh, I don't mind... really, I don't.

MONA. Well, I mind.

EDNA. (*To* MONA.) I'm sorry I made you mind. I didn't mean to.

STELLA. That uniform you wore in here looked a helluva lot better on you than that thing does. (*Drags* SISSY *out.*) C'mon, Sissy, let's get that beer.

EDNA. (*To* STELLA *as* SHE *exits.*) Oh, but that's my work dress. (*To* JOANNE.) I wear it practic'ly every day... it's so old and...

JOANNE. Comfortable?

EDNA. (*Smiles.*) Well, yes it is. I feel so much more relaxed an'... at home in it than this, but...

JOANNE. You glowed brighter than anyone in the place.

EDNA. Glowed? (SHE *beams.*) Did I really? You make me sound like the sun ... or a movie star. Nobody ever told me I glowed before. I think I will change then since nobody really minds. (*Starts to go.*) I'll be back ... don't anybody go away. (SHE *smiles from ear to ear.*) Glowin'?! (SHE *exits into the backroom.*)

MONA. That was a terrible thing to tell her. Stella will tease her 'til she cries.

JOANNE. Too bad you can't accept the truth about yourself as simply as Edna Louise there.

MONA. Well, I've been travellin' an' my dress is all ...

JOANNE. I'm not referring to your dress and you know it.

MONA. No, I don't know it. I have no idea of what you are referrin' to ... do you, Juanita?

JUANITA. I don't understand anythin' that's been goin' on here tonight.

MONA. I'm sorry, but your point of reference seems to have just passed right on over our heads. (*Smiles.*)

JOANNE. How convenient for you, Mona. You know I drove through Marfa on the way here. Too bad, isn't it, how Reata has just fallen flat on its face like that. It was nothing but a big phony front all along.

MONA. Well, you didn't expect it to stay a mystery forever, did you? It may not be there any longer in real life, but it is still as it was in my memory.

JOANNE. Memories slip away.

MONA. I have Jimmy Dean an' all my photographs. They won't let me forget.

JUANITA. You leave her alone, you hear?...Communist!

MONA. Tell him, Juanita ... Tell him I have nothin' to hide.

JUANITA. So long as you know it, there's no reason to have to convince anybody else.

JOANNE. You mean as long as you've forced yourself to believe it's true.

JUANITA. I believe in God and His Son...the Holy Bible an' it's teachin's...and I believe in Sidney an' the joy an' happiness he brought into my life. Those beliefs are all that I have. They *are* my life and the truth is my belief in them.

SISSY. (*Entering with* STELLA.) Beer's outside on the curb for when ya want it.

STELLA. (*Holds up a bourbon bottle.*) An' I brought along a bottle of bourbon for the hard core drinkers.

JUANITA. On the curb?! You can't leave it sittin' out there on the curb. Bring it on inside an' hide it there behin' the counter.

SISSY. I can't believe it ... the devil's done won you over. (SISSY *goes out and drags it in.*)

JUANITA. Close them doors an' pull down them shades.

STELLA. We'll suffocate, for Chrissake.

JUANITA. Somebody from my prayer club may drive by.

SISSY. Just cause they all drink behin' closed doors don't mean we have to.

MONA. Did you see Jimmy Dean out there?

SISSY. Luke said he never come back from the train sidin'.

MONA. Juanita, I told you somethin' awful would happen, an' it has ... I know it.

JUANITA. I'll go on over by the tracks an' see if I can round him up ... You just calm yourself down an' try to have a good time.

JOANNE. (*To* STELLA.) I'll have some of that bourbon if you don't mind. (SHE *goes to* STELLA. JUANITA *grabs her arm as* SHE *passes.*)

JUANITA. You are dead wrong about Sidney. He was very upset about what he had to do ... it hurt him straight up till the day he died ... of a heart attack. (SHE *exits.*)

STELLA. (*Handing* JOANNE *a glass of bourbon.*) I'm very curious about this thing you had done. What do they do? ... I mean is it just plastic parts they *glue* all over you, or what?

JOANNE. It's a psychological process ... something you couldn't possibly understand. (*To* SISSY.) There's nothin' I can mix with this?

SISSY. (*Gestures toward the backroom.*) Toilet water.

JOANNE. I'll drink it straight.

EDNA. (*Entering buttoning up her old uniform.*) I'm spendin' so much time changin' and re-changin', I'm missin' the whole party.

STELLA. What the hell happened to that fancy dress you drug all the way here?

EDNA. I prefer this one after all ... it's more comfortable.

STELLA. Talk about your weirdos.

MONA. I told you she'd make fun of her.

JOANNE. I propose a toast. Everybody got a drink? Stella and Sissy are taken care of ... Edna Louise?

EDNA. Oh, I don't drink. It might have a bad influence on the baby.

STELLA. Ain't she a dip though? Christ, I wonder why the hell she even bothers to get up in the mornin'.

EDNA. (*Embarrassed smile, then suddenly blurts out.*) I'll have one! ... please.

JOANNE. One beer for the little lady with the radiant glow. Mona? ... a little pick-me-up to help refresh your memory?

MONA. An Orange Crush will suit me just fine. (*Goes to the counter to fix it.*)

SISSY. This operation you had done ... did it hurt?

JOANNE. Not until years later. I had a delayed reaction.

SISSY. You mean you regret it?

JOANNE. Only when I think about it.

SISSY. Can you ...? You know ...

JOANNE Have sex? ... Can.

STELLA. And?

JOANNE. Have ... on occassion.

SISSY. Me, too ... any occassion I can. (*Laughs.*) Holy shit, I nearly forgot...hey...hey, guess what...?The Queen of the Dixie Rollerrink is gonna make her big comeback. Whattaya think about that, huh?

STELLA. Sissy, at your age?

SISSY. What the hell's the matter with my age? (*Adjust her boobs.*) They're still as bouncy as they ever were.

JOANNE. (*Goes toward* SISSY.) Can I feel? They could be just jello for all we know.

SISSY. (*Pulling away.*) Stay away from my boobs ... pervert. (*Laughs it off.*)

STELLA. What are ya gonna do, join up with one of them Roller Derbies?

SISSY. Nope ... the Ice Capades.

STELLA. Ice Capades? ... Shit, you'd fall flat on your ass roller skatin' on ice.

EDNA. Oh, how excitin'! Will you get to wear one of them fancy costumes with sparkles an' feathers all over it?

SISSY. You'd better believe it, little mama.

STELLA. (*Laughing.*) Sissy, you've always been such a damn panic.

SISSY. Million cheap laughs. (*Drinks.*)

JOANNE. (*Announcing.*) Everybody finally ready for the toast? As vice president of the "Disciples of James Dean" ... I am still vice president? I mean ... I haven't been black-balled since I've been *de* ... parted?

STELLA. Hell, who cares ... I wanna drink!

JOANNE. (*Raising her glass.*) To James Dean ... long live the dead.

(MONA (THEN) *enters from outside and goes to the back room door. At this point both groups become involved in the same meeting. Only* STELLA *and* EDNA *will double as "then" and "now" switching ages as their lines indicate. Neither group acknowledges or is aware of the other except them.*)

STELLA. (*Laughing.*) Long live the dead. That's a good one. (*To* MONA (THEN)) Hey, Mona, we're gonna have a meetin' ain't we?

MONA (THEN). In just a minute, Stella. (*Calls off.*) Joe ... Sissy ... Stella May an' Edna Louise are here ... It's time to start the meetin'.

JOANNE. Everybody still remember the ritual of the meeting?

EDNA. I do! ... I do! I have all the minutes in my notebook.

(SISSY (THEN) *enters wearing her club jacket and carrying an arm-full of beer.* JOE *follows.*)

MONA (THEN). You sure Juanita's gone?

SISSY (THEN). She left for her prayer club meetin' 'bout fifteen minutes ago. (*Goes behind the counter with the beer.*) I'm gonna cool these beers off in the crushed ice, if anybody wants one.

JOANNE. Mona, what do you think?

JOE. We can make it work, Mona ... I know we can.

MONA (THEN). (*Ignoring him.*) I think we should bring the meetin' to order.

SISSY. Come on Mona, whattaya say?

MONA. If you want to ... I'll participate.

(STELLA *cheers.* EDNA *grins and applauds.*)

STELLA. Yahoo! ... This is gonna be a Goddamm panic ... Hey ... Hey, I wanna wear my club jacket. (*Goes for it*)

EDNA. Me too! (*Puts hers on.*) Mona, where's yours?

(JOE *hands* MONA (THEN) *her jacket.*)

MONA. At home ... My bus was late gettin' in an' I didn't have time to go on by an' get it.

SISSY. I lost mine years ago.

JOANNE. Me too.

SISSY. You bet your ass you did, honey. (SISSY *and* JOANNE *laugh.*)

JOANNE. Now, the song was the first thing, that much I remember. Sissy always led and the rest of us followed the bouncing boobs.

SISSY. Would you just keep my boobs outta this.

STELLA. (*Roars.*) Hell, that's impossible.

SISSY (THEN). This all that's gonna be showin' up tonight?

MONA. I suppose we're the only ones who cared enough to remember.

STELLA. Well, I'm here an' I wanna sing!

SISSY (THEN). O.K. everybody ... gather 'roun' an' follow the bouncin' boobs.

(THEY *all gather together as one group. Both* SISSYs *conduct them as they sing to the tune of "The Eyes of Texas."* SISSY *starts to laugh.* STELLA *forgets the words, etc.*)

EVERYONE.
> The eyes of James Dean are upon us,
> All the live long day.
> The eyes of James Dean are upon us,
> You cannot get away.
> You might think you can escape them
> from night to early in the morn.
> The eyes of James Dean are upon us
> 'Til Gab'rel blows his horn.

(THEY *applaud, giggle, etc.*)

STELLA. (*Wiping away a tear.*) This is such a panic!

MONA (THEN). Edna Louise, would you read the minutes of the last meetin'?

EDNA. (*Then.*) (*Standing and very official.*) I have to announce, a little embarrassed, that the minutes of the last meetin' got accidentally eaten up by my dog, Rosie. (*Quickly.*) But I think I remember most of what happened in my head if you would like me to speak it.

STELLA. I thought you said you had them all written down in your notebook.

EDNA. (*Flipping through her notebook.*) I have nearly every one, I guess, but the *last* one.

MONA. We will dispense with the readin' of the minutes due to not havin' 'em.

EDNA. (*Then.*) But I have them up here. (*Points to her head.*)

STELLA. (*Then.*) Too bad Rosie didn't eat your head instead.

MONA (THEN). Stella May, quit pickin' on Edna Louise an' get yourself serious.

STELLA. (*Then.*) I *am* serious ... but she's so damn dumb, that's all .. I can't stand people who are dumb.

MONA. Sissy, would you give the treasurer's report?

SISSY (THEN). We had eighteen dollars an' thirty-six cents, but we spent twelve dollars an' thirteen cents to buy the emblems for our new club jackets ... so that leaves about ...

SISSY. ... Six dollars an' somethin' that we gave to Mona to buy a floral wreath to lay on his grave ... so kiddos ... we're broke.

MONA (THEN). Pictures for the collection. Does anybody have one we don't already have, to hang on the wall?

SISSY (THEN). Mona found her a whole magazine full of 'em when she was away at college. There's a full page color one of him with no shirt on that's just dreamy.

SISSY. Christ, Mona, you've got every one that's ever been taken of him.

SISSY (THEN). Go get it Mona, they'll just die.

(MONA *goes into the backroom to get it.*)

STELLA. (*Excited.*) I got a dandy one! (SHE *chuckles as* SHE *goes to her purse to get a large envelope.*) Careful not to get your fingers all over it now 'cause it cost me an arm an' a leg on the black market. Girl's this is gonna knock your eyeballs right outta their sockets.

MONA (THEN). (*At the door with the magazine behind her.*) Are you ready?

STELLA. (*Producing an eight by ten glossy from the envelope at the same time* MONA (THEN) *holds out the full-page photo of Dean.*) DA...da! The real James Dean, stands up!

SISSY. My God, would you look at the size of that thing!

SISSY (THEN). (*Squeels.*) Ain't that the sexiest thing you've ever seen?

MONA. (*Moves away.*) That's disgustin!

JOANNE. You didn't think so at one time, Mona.

MONA. That is not a picture of him!

SISSY. It sure as hell ain't my Aunt Sally.

SISSY (THEN). There any of him in there in a bathin' suit?

MONA. He would never let anybody take a picture of him like that.

EDNA. Is that a tree branch in his hand, or what?

SISSY. Edna?! . . . an' you've got six kids?!

(EDNA *screams with embarrassment when she realizes what it is.*)

STELLA. No wonder you're holdin' on to his memory, with a monument like that.

MONA. Stop all this filthy talk! That is not a picture of James Dean.

JOANNE. Mona, are you sure. (*Pulls her toward the photo.*) Look closer. It was dark that night. You could be mistaken.

SISSY (THEN). (*Grabs at the magazine.*) God, there's one I missed.

MONA (THEN). Careful, you'll rip it.

MONA. (*Grabs the photo and tears it up.*) Stop this!

SISSY. Hey, don't do that. I'll take it if you don't . . . (*It's too late.*)

STELLA. Gimme them pieces, maybe I can paste 'em back together or . . . (*Tosses them up in the air.*) Aw, shit!

MONA (THEN). Does anybody have anything they want to share with the rest of us? Stories or little known facts that will enlighten our lives about James Dean?

JOANNE. Mona, why don't you tell us that story of how you were chosen to be the Virgin Mona of the Texas Testament.

EDNA. (*Then.*) Mona, tell us about Marfa an' bein' on that movie with him.

SISSY. Wouldn't be a meetin' without *that* story.

STELLA. Ya, Mona . . . C'mon.

MONA. (*Moves up to the door.*) I'm concerned about Jimmy Dean.

STELLA. You just wanna be begged, that's all.

MONA (THEN). Well, you all know how everyone in town was just buzzin' when it was announced over the radio they were lookin' for people to be in it.

STELLA. (*Then.*) God, I'm so jealous of you for gettin' to go I could spit.

SISSY. Christ, if I had seen that picture then instead of now, I woulda told Lester T. to stick his drive-in picture show up his nose an' crawled over to Marfa on my hands an' knees.

STELLA. Mona, c'mon back on in here an' tell us again how it happened.

EDNA.   Please, Mona, I'd just love to hear it again.

MONA. (*A smile to* EDNA.) You really would? (EDNA *smiles back and nods her head.*) Well, alright. (STELLA *cheers.*) It was like a regular parade. People from all over these parts headed for Marfa, bumper to bumper, to be in that movie. Joe borrowed his . . . (SHE *stops short.*)

JOANNE. That's all right, Mona . . . it was *his*, then.

MONA/MONA (THEN). Joe borrowed his mama's Buick and . . .

MONA. . . . right after work we drove off into the

sunset, laughin' an' gigglin' an' pretendin' like it was the end of a movie. It hadn't even begun yet, that was the funny part. We were playin' the endin' an' the beginnin' was yet to come. I pretended I was Natalie Wood and Joe . . .

JOANNE. I was James Dean . . . pretendin' I wasn't Joseph Qualley.

MONA/MONA (THEN). There were nearly four thousand . . .

MONA (THEN). . . . people in that small town when We got there. All the rooms in the Paisano Hotel were filled-up, so Joe an' I had to sleep in the Buick along the side of the road.

SISSY. (*Singing.*) Oh, little town of Bethlehem . . .

STELLA. (*Laughs.*) Oh, Sissy, be quiet.

MONA/MONA (THEN). Next mornin' . . .

MONA (THEN). . . . after I had washed up in the sink of the gas station across the road, nearly rubbin' my skin off with Boraxo an' paper towels . . .

MONA. . . . I was sittin' in the back seat of the Buick pourin' lilac perfune all over to get rid of the smell of the Boraxo, when I saw "him" walkin' down the road, right towards me.

STELLA. (*Then.*) My God, I need me another beer before I faint.

SISSY (THEN). Get me another too, would ya, Stel.

(STELLA *goes behind the counter.*)

MONA. . . . an' he stopped right next to the car, lookin' in his pocket for somethin'. There was a cigarette danglin' from out of the corner of his mouth, so I took a chance that a match was what he was huntin' for and I leaned out the car window an' says ... "I've got a match, if that's what you're needin'." He sort of smiled an' took the matches just like he had been livin' in Texas all his life.

MONA (THEN). (*Taking a lace handkerchief out of her dress pocket and unfolds it.*) And here are the matches that he touched. (SISSY (THEN), STELLA *and* EDNA *squeel and lean over them.*) Careful now ... you might wipe the fingerprints off.

MONA. I had those matches for the longest time afterwards. I finally had to sell them to a woman in California for three hundred dollars to get money to buy braces for Jimmy Dean's teeth.

JOE. (*Producing a cigarette butt from his overalls pocket.*) I found a cigarette butt layin' in the road ... it's a Chesterfield, the same brand he smokes.

SISSY (THEN). And eighty million other people, too.

MONA (THEN). Hush up, Joe.

JOE. Well, I was there, too, you know.

MONA (THEN). (*Ignoring him.*) When he lit his cigarette and I looked up into them deep-set, sky-blue eyes ... I could see myself, clear as lookin' in a mirror. It was at that very moment I knew somethin' was gonna happen to change my whole life.

EDNA. (*Swooning, getting drunk.*) This story reminds me of a movie I saw one time.

MONA. Later on at the place where they were pickin' people to be in the movie ... an' they picked me ... me, out of all them hundreds of others ... I knew for certain!

JOE. They said I didn't look like "Texas" enough. What the hell does "Texas" look like, anyhow?

MONA (THEN). They were lookin' for types. You just weren't the right type, that's all.

STELLA. Ya know, I look for you every time I see that movie on T.V. an' I never see you.

MONA. Elizabeth Taylor's head keeps gettin' in the way ... but, I'm there, mostly behin' her left ear in that scene where she first arrives from her papa's plantation in Virginia ... an' they have that big barbecue picnic scene. She gets real hot an' starts to faint, grabbin' onto the branch of a mesquite tree for support ... right as the camera comes close to her at that point ... you can see me peekin' out from behin' her left ear.

MONA (THEN). I felt like such a celebrity the way they were all fussin' over me.

JOE. Mona, you sound like you was the only one there ... there were so many people, I could hardly even find you.

MONA (THEN). Joe, if you aren't interested in listenin' ... you can leave. (SHE *goes on building to a desperate frenzy.*) That night I laid there in the back seat of the Buick and kept thinkin' about how I was chosen above all them thousands of others ... starin' out the window at the millions of stars an' the outline of that beautiful house way off in the distance. Suddenly, one of those stars exploded, burst away from all the millions of others an' fell from the sky ... landin' right behin' the house ... behin' the front of Reata. I leaned over the seat to point it out to Joe, but he had tramped off somewhere, all mad 'cause he wasn't chosen, too.

JOE. I didn't tramp off mad. I just wanted to be alone

MONA. I pulled my blanket aroun' my shoulders an' started to walk to where the star had fallen to earth. I walked past the front gate down the road to the house. It was so quiet and still . . . the only sound was comin' from a far away train, blowin' its whistle an' chuggin' off into the night. When I got to the front porch, this voice comin' outta nowhere says, "Isn't it a little late to be callin' on your neighbors?" It was him. I knew it. I knew it the first minute I heard his voice. Then he said, "Don't just stand there bein' unfriendly. Come on up on the porch an' sit a spell." As I moved up the stairs, I reminded him that I was the one who gave him a match that mornin' . . . an he thanked me again. We spent that whole entire night together . . . . until the sun started to peek out from over the edge of the earth, turnin' the sky into the brightest red I ever saw.

JOE. Mona, what are you sayin'?!

MONA (THEN). (*Sharply to* JOE.) We walked together to the gate an' he thanked me for sharin' the night with him an' then we both walked away in separate directions.

STELLA. (*Then.*) You shared the same night with James Dean?

JOE. Mona, no! . . . That's not the way it was an' you know it.

SISSY (THEN). Mona . . . you never told me that part of the story before. I'm your friend . . . you're best friend and you never told me.

JOE. She never told you 'cause it's a lie.

MONA (THEN). It's not a lie . . . it's true.

STELLA. (*Then.*) Maybe it was just a dream ... It had to be dream.

MONA (THEN). (*Angrily.*) It wasn't a dream!

JOE. Why are you doin' this to me, Mona?

MONA (THEN). I'm not doin' nothin' but tellin' the entire story, at last.

JOE. (*Storms to the backroom.*) It's not the *true* story.

SISSY (THEN). (*Follows him.*) Then what really happened then, Joe? Joe ... come back here.

MONA (THEN). Don't listen to him, Sissy ... He doesn't know what happened ... he wasn't there!

EDNA. (*Then.*) (*The innocent.*) I'm so happy for you, Mona.

MONA. That morning we left because Joe had to have his mama's Buick back. (*With a glance to* JOANNE.) Remember? (*To the others.*) And I never saw James Dean again.

JUANITA. (*Entering hurriedly.*) Turn on the radio, quick! Somethin's happenin' over in the southwest.

MONA. What is it?

JUANITA. Lightnin', I saw lightnin'. Praise the Lord.

SISSY. It's prob'ly just heat lightnin'.

JUANITA. (*Goes to the radio behind the counter.*) No, I think I heard thunder, too. (*Distant thunder.*)

STELLA. Aw, shit! ... an' I just had the car washed, too.

MONA. Where's Jimmy Dean? ... Didn't you find him out there?

JUANITA. I couldn't find him no place. I saw that lightnin' an' rushed on back here as fast as I could ... Praise the Lord.

MONA. This is all your fault, Juanita ... if you'd have kept an eye on him, none of this would have happened. (SHE *rushes outside calling for him.*)

JUANITA. Ain't nothin' happened, yet. (SHE *fools with the radio dial.*) This is the only station that seems to be comin' in clear.

(*The radio is broadcasting to a revival meeting. It underscores the next scene faintly. Thunder is heard coming closer.*)

JUANITA. It's comin' closer, do you hear? (SHE *rushes outside.*)

SISSY (THEN). (*Entering.*) Mona, I can't get over you keepin' that a secret from me.

MONA (THEN). I never figured anyone would ever believe me.

SISSY. (THEN.)   Why's Joe keep sayin' it's a lie?

MONA (THEN). He's jealous, that's why ... jealous because our god called to me.

SISSY (THEN). God?!

MONA (THEN). He is out god, isn't he? ... and we're his disciples.

EDNA. (*Then.*) Not for real? ... he's not our real god, is he?

MONA (THEN). I read in a movie magazine how he's the god of teenagers everywhere ... that he's really us up there on that movie screen showin' us the answers to all our questions ... did you know that?

SISSY (THEN). Mona, that's crazy.

MONA (THEN). No, it isn't! ... "They" tell us there is only one God ... why should we believe them? How do we even know he existed? (*To* EDNA.) Have you ever seen him? Have you?

EDNA. (*Then.*) I've seen him on the walls in church ... and in my prayer book.

MONA (THEN). But you've never seen him for real.

SISSY (THEN). Mona, stop all this craziness.

MONA (THEN). James Dean is alive. We *know* he exists.

JOE. (*Entering obviously shaken.*) Mona, what are you up to?

MONA (THEN). I'm up to tellin' the truth ... I have to tell the truth.

JOE. Then tell it, dammit!

MONA. (THEN). (*Forced.*) He . . . He made love to me!

STELLA. (*Then.*) Who did?

MONA (THEN). James Dean made love to me that night ... and I can prove it.

SISSY. (THEN. You're outta your head! ... There's no way you can prove such a crazy story like that.

MONA (THEN). The doctors can ... They examined me. They can prove it. His child is inside me. The son of James Dean is inside my body.

(*A deafening clap of thunder and lightening.*)

SISSY (THEN). (*Shocked.*) I don't believe you.

JUANITA. It's comin' right toward us ... he heard, he heard my prayers.

MONA. (*Entering the store.*) He couldn't have just disappeared into nowhere.

JOE. Mona, is it true? ... are you really goin' to have a baby? (*Grabs her.*)

MONA (THEN). (*Pulling away.*) "His" baby! (*To* STELLA.) You believe me, don't you?

JUANITA. Oh, God, let me believe in you.

MONA (THEN). (*Grabbing* EDNA.) You believe me?!

EDNA. (*Then.*) (*Falling to her knees.*) I believe ... I believe in James Dean.

EDNA. (*Grabs her stomach.*) I'm sick.

STELLA. (*Rushing to her.*) She's drunk, for Chrissake. (SHE *leads her to the bathroom.*)

RADIO ANNOUNCER. We interrupt this program to bring you an important news bulletin ...

(*The sound of a car starting up and pulling away.*)

JUANITA. (*Outside.*) Oh, my God! . . . Mona! . . . Mona, come out here, quick. It's Jimmy Dean ... he's drivin' away in that yellow sports car.

MONA. (*Rushing to the door.*) No! ...it can't be ... He doesn't even know how to drive! (*Outside.*) Jimmy Dean ... Jimmy Dean, you come on back here!

(SISSY *starts to laugh mysteriously.* JOANNE *goes to her purse.*)

JOANNE. I could swear I took the keys out of the ignition. (SHE *doesn't find them.*)

RADIO ANNOUNCER. One of Hollywood's brightest young stars was killed early this evening along California State Highway 466. A head-on collision took the life of James Dean ...

MONA. (THEN). No! . . . not James Dean! . . . not James Dean!

(SISSY (THEN) *and* JOE *react in silent disbelief.*)

JUANITA. Somebody call up the Highway Patrol. Maybe they can stop him before he hurts himself.

MONA. How did he ever get that car started?

JOANNE. I must have left the keys in it by mistake.

SISSY. (*Calmly getting another beer.*) You'd be shocked by what that boy can do.

MONA. What are you talkin' about? He can't even tie his shoes by himself.

JOANNE. Can't tie his shoes? What are you talkin' about? (*Into phone.*) Hello? . . . Highway Patrol . . .

JUANITA. He must have learned how to drive from watchin' Luke over at the Texaco.

MONA. (*Angrily.*) I told you, Juanita! . . . I told you!

STELLA. (*Entering from the backroom.*) Christ, she's sick as a dog. Threw up all over the ladies room. All she had was one beer . . . one beer.

JOANNE. (*Into phone.*) A yellow Porsche . . . P-O-R-S-C-H-E.

MONA. (*To* SISSY.) What did you mean by that mysterious remark of yours?

JUANITA. You don't pay her no mind, you hear? She's drunk an' don't know what she's talkin' about.

JOANNE. That's right, the Kressmont five-and-dime . . . thank you. (SHE *hangs up.*) The Highway Patrol's on their way to pick him up. They'll call as soon as they know something. (*To* MONA.) Nothing will happen. Don't worry.

MONA. I *do* worry. I worry all the time about him. I can't let him outta my sight for a minute. It wasn't my fault he turned out that way. All the doctors said so. It was the shock of... (*Gestures to the shrine.*) his dyin'... it jostled my insides an' created a... a...

SISSY. A son!

MONA. (*Directly to* JOANNE.) Who is a moron!

JOANNE. (*Stunned.*) What?!

MONA. A moron I have to hide away from everybody because...

SISSY. (*Controlling herself.*) Mona, shut your mouth.

JUANITA. Mona, that's enough.

MONA. It was somebody in this town, I'll bet, who put him up to this... they're always puttin' him up to crazy things to make him look foolish so's they can laugh an'...

SISSY. They don't laugh at...

MONA. They do laugh!... because they're jealous. (SHE *goes to the shrine.*) They're everyone of 'em, jealous!

SISSY (THEN). I feel so funny inside... like it was the end of the world or somethin'... I wanna cry but I'm too scared. Hold my hand, Joe... I need someone to hold on to.

(HE *takes her hand.*)

JOE. Hold my other hand, Mona. (HE *holds out his hand to her.* SHE *starts to take it but changes her mind and moves away.*)

STELLA. (*Then.*) I think we should all kneel down

an' pray or somethin' . . . don't you Mona?

JOE. Mona, hold my hand . . . please?

STELLA. (*Then.*) Or light candles! . . . We could light dozens of candles. That'd be so pretty, don't you think?

MONA (THEN). No, we won't let him die . . . his son . . . his son will carry on in his place.

JOE. Mona, don't . . . it's not *his* son.

MONA (THEN). It *was* James Dean. It was him that night on the front porch of Reata. When his son is born you'll see . . . he'll look exactly like him . . . exactly! (SHE *goes outside.*)

SISSY (THEN). Mona . . . (SHE *follows her out.*) where are you goin'? . . .

(EDNA *enters unnoticed and stands in the doorway.*)

MONA. (*Holding a picture of James Dean.*) His hair should have been blond like his father's . . . not brown. (*Touches the hair on the picture.*) It was blond . . . blond as a dusty sunrise.

EDNA. We tried to dye it blond once, remember? But it turned green instead.

JUANITA. (*Going to her.*) Are you alright now, Edna Louise?

EDNA. I'm a little shaky, but I suppose I will survive.

JUANITA. Come, sit down. (SHE *takes* EDNA *to a chair.*)

JOE. (*Alone at the door,*) It wasn't him, Mona.

JOANNE. (*Going to* MONA.) Mona, I'm sorry . . . are they sure?

JOE. Please tell the truth, Mona . . . please.

MONA. They're positive.

JOE. The truth, Mona. (HE *exits outside.*)

JOANNE. Didn't they suggest any kind of therapy . . . specialists?

MONA. You think they can cut his sickness away like they did yours? Yours was easy to remedy. For him there is no cure. His mind will never mature . . . never catch up to the rest of his body. He'll be a child forever.

SISSY. Just like you always wanted to be . . . right, Mona?

JOANNE. Sissy, that's enough.

SISSY. No, it ain't enough. I'm sick of all this . . . this crap of hers.

JUANITA. She's drunk. She doesn't know what she's sayin'.

SISSY. I know exactly what I'm sayin', thank you very much. (*To* JOANNE.) What kind of car did I hear you say you was drivin'?

JOANNE. Porsche, P-O-R-

SISSY. I know how to spell, thank you. That's the kinda car James Dean drove all the time, ain't it?

JOANNE. What the hell are you up to, Sissy?

SISSY. I ain't up to nothin' . . . it's just a strange kinda co-incidence if you ask me . . . the same night, twenty years later . . . same car . . .

JOANNE. Are you trying to say I left those keys in the car, intentionally, just for him to find?

SISSY. I ain't sayin' nothin'.

JOANNE. Well, you sure as hell are "insinuating"

I'm somehow involved in all this.

SISSY. Ain't ya?

MONA. (*To* JOANNE.) That's why you really came back here, isn't it?

JOANNE. Sissy, what the hell are you tryin' to do ?

MONA. You thought you could force me to say it's not true, didn't you?...into sayin' he isn't the son of James Dean at all, didn't you?

JOANNE. How the hell was I supposed to know he'd drive off in my car?

MONA. *His* car!...James Dean's car.

JOANNE. My car! (*Moves away.*) Mona, you're not making sense.

MONA. Well your little trick will not work. They'll stop him in time.

SISSY. Don't be too positive. What's that sayin' you're always rattlin' off, Juanita?..."God works in mysterious ways."

JUANITA. Don't you go blamin' God for any of this.

SISSY. Well, somebody's got to take the blame ...Joe says it isn't him...oops, "her"...an' you say it wasn't God...then who was it? (*To* EDNA.) Edna, honey...was it you?

EDNA. (*Flustered.*) Me?...no...I...

JUANITA. Nobody's to blame. Everythin' will turn out just fine. (*To* MONA.) God's watchin' over him, honey.

SISSY. (*Toasts with her beer bottle.*) Good ol' God.

JUANITA. It wouldn't hurt none for you to say a little prayer neither.

SISSY. I ain't prayin' these days. I gave it up for Lent.

JOANNE. When did you stop, Sissy ... When Lester T. walked out on you?

STELLA. Sissy, he didn't?!

SISSY. (*To* JOANNE.) Look, sister ... or mister, or whatever the hell you are ... don't you go startin' in on me. 'cause you don't know nothin'.

JOANNE. I know a lot more than you think.

STELLA. Sissy, did he really?

SISSY. No, he did not! He got himself a job over there in Arabia ... or Lebanon ... one of them damn places ... wildcattin' for some big oil company

STELLA. How long's he been gone?

SISSY. Two ... three years. He says he wants me to come over ... says he misses me like hell ... but I can't live over there with all them foreigners. He writes me all the time, though ... sometimes twice a week.

JOANNE. When's he coming back?

SISSY. When he's damn good an' ready! (*To* STELLA.) You know that bastard's makin' nearly a hundred dollars a day over there ... (*Laughs.*) Why the hell come back. I told him ... "don't worry none about me .. I'll keep." (*To* JOANNE) So there! (*Raises her bottle upwards.*) Up yours!

JOANNE. A very believable explanation ... but not very accurate. (*Goes to get herself a drink.*)

SISSY. Look, I don't know what you *think* you know, but ...

JOANNE. I know what *he* told me.

SISSY. Lester T. (*Laughs.*) Where'd you meet him ... behin' some gravestone somewhere?

JOANNE. Oklahoma City . . . a couple years back.

SISSY. Oklahoma City?! (*Laughs.*) How the hell could he be in Oklahoma City when . . .

JOANNE. It's true.

SISSY. Prove it!

JOANNE. (*Directly to her.*) Sissy, let's just say I know . . . an' leave it at that, O.K.?

SISSY. No, you started this an' I wanna hear. I ain't afraid of your lies.

JOANNE. (*Gives in.*) Don't say I didn't warn you.

SISSY. O.K., I'm warned. What the hell were you doin' in Oklahoma City, anyhow?

JOANNE. Actually, I went there with the intention of seeing you . . . I had heard you were living there and thought I'd show up on your doorstep, and surprise you . . . but, somewhere around the city limits, I lost my courage and ended up in some downtown bar instead . . . I'd had one or two drinks and was up on this platform leaning on the juke-box singing along to some record that was playing . . . you remember, like we used to . . . The record plays and you move your mouth and pretend you're Eydie Gorme.

SISSY. You can move your mouth an pretend all you want 'cause you don't know crap from Christmas.

JOANNE. We'll see. Anyhow, there I was, singing away to myself when I glanced out over the crowd and floating over a cloud of cigarette smoke was this face . . . a face from the past that jumped out to jar loose a whole lot of locked up memories. He sure was giving me the once-over. His eyes were glued to my boobs just like the first time we en-

countered each other. He smiled that big dumb smile
of his and came on over to the juke-box ... said
he had to tell me how much he loved my singin' ...
that I sounded just like Eydie Gorme. He invited
me to join him for a drink, which I did ... bourbon
and water, wasn't it, Sissy? (SISSY *turns away.*)
Well, that one led to another, and another, and
then he began to pour out the woeful tale of the
wife he left behind him, the "Ex-Queen of the Dixie
Roller Rink" from McCarthy, Texas who had boobs
the size of watermelons. He really thought she was
"something" ... thought so since their high school
days when they'd get together for "hanky-panky"
in the old graveyard. He was crazy over them watermelons of hers ... They really won him over ...
They got married eventually and were living happily-
ever-after, until ... one day the watermelons just
disappeared ... went away, and ... so did ... (SHE
stops suddenly with remorse.) I'm sorry, Sissy ... I
went too far.

STELLA. Don't stop now, for Chrissake. I wanna
know where the hell the watermelons went.

MONA. Sissy, I told you not to marry him ... that
he never really loved you.

SISSY. (*Sharply to her.*) He did too love me ... he
worshipped me. (*To* JOANNE.) He told you that,
didn't he? ... He told you he loved me?

JOANNE. (*Simply.*) Yes, he ... did ...

SISSY. (*Squeezing her arms to her body,* SHE
turns away.) He said that it was repulsive to him ...
that it disgusted him. (*Lowering her head.*) Oh, God
... I begged them not to take them, but they said

it would spread ... that it would ...

JUANITA. Oh, Sissy, I'm so sorry ... You should have told us ...

SISSY. What did you want me to do? ... run in, rip open my dress an' yell, "Hi everybody, I'm back ... an' look, no more tits?" I was too scared to say anythin' to anybody ... (*Getting emotional.*) Lester T ... he ... he would fall asleep every night with his head against 'em ... he loved them so much ... more than he did me, I guess. He was one helluva lover though . . .every night . . two, three time we'd make love. After the operation it dwindled down to once a week, an' then ... no more. Even with the lights out, I'd feel his hands want to reach out for what wasn't there. I cried all the time 'cause one day I knew he wouldn't want me no more ... an' the day came ... an' he went. (*Pause.*) Did he ... make love to you?

JOANNE. He wanted to ... begged and pleaded with me to go off someplace with him, and I ... I considered it ... for revenge ... considered letting him have his way and then ... (*Starting to laugh.*) Surprise him with my true identy. God, I would have given anything to see the look on his face. (*Laughs louder.*) "Guess who? ... It's me!"

SISSY. (*Starting to laugh also.*) Why the hell, didn't you?

JOANNE. It all didn't seem to matter anymore. He ended up buying me six or seven drinks and going on home alone.

SISSY. Serves him right, the bastard! God, it feels good to laugh. I haven't laughed this hard in years. (*Moves to the door.* "They" always laughed though, at Sissy with the giant boobs ... for years I had to lug them damn things aroun' for them all to pinch an' squeeze an' get their jollies. That's all they wanted ... they never gave a rat's-ass for me. (SHE *goes out the door.*) Hey ... hey, everybody out there in McCarthy, Texas . . . guess what?! . . .They're rubber! . Sissy's got rubber tits!

JUANITA. (*Rushing to her.*) Sissy, get in here!

SISSY. I don't care anymore.

MONA. (*To* JOANNE.) I hope you are pleased with yourself now that you have humiliated her. (*To* SISSY.) Sissy, I'm sorry.

SISSY. (*Pulling away from her.*) I don't want your pity, Mona. (*To* JOANNE.) I sure pulled the rubber over their eyes these last coupla' years, didn't I? ... not real tits at all, just ... re-treads.

STELLA. (*Joins her laughter.*) Re-treads?!

MONA. Sissy, that's not funny.

SISSY. Whattaya want me to do, cry? ... I cried enough ... for three Goddamm years, I cried. (*Goes behind the counter.*) I need me another beer.

MONA. (*To* JOANNE.) You may leave the party at any time. Do not feel you have to remain until the end on our account.

JOANNE. I can't leave without my car.

MONA. They will be returnin' "it," an' Jimmy Dean anytime now ... It really makes me sick to my stomach to think that people can be so cruel. (SISSY *starts to laugh.*) What is so funny, now?

SISSY. You. (*Mimicking her.*) "It makes me sick to my stomach to think people can be so cruel."

MONA. (*Goes to the phone to ignore her.*) I just don't understand what is takin' them so long. Maybe

the phone is out of order, along with everythin'
else.

SISSY. (*Goes after her.*) There's nothin' wrong
with the Goddamm phone. (*Grabs it from her.*) He's
gone!

MONA. (*Innocently.*) Well, I know that he's gone,
Heavens, I'm not blind am I?

SISSY. Then why do you think everybody else
is?

MONA. I don't understand your point.

SISSY. Stop all the crap, Mona ... He's run away
... Flew the coop ... Gone!

MONA. (*Small laugh.*) He couldn't run away ...
he doesn't even know what it means ... He doesn't
know how to do anythin' without me to help him.
(*Moves away.*) He's only a child ... a poor helpless ...

SISSY. That's what you are, for Chrissake, not
him! He's all grown up, Mona ... Open your damn
eyes an' see it.

MONA. His mind isn't ... his mind is like a ...

SISSY. The only thing wrong with his mind is
that he couldn't make it up soon enough to get
the hell outta here ... away from you an' your crazy
ideas about him. He finally made it up, Mona ... He's
gone!

MONA. No, he couldn't decide somethin' like that
by himself.

SISSY. I helped him!

MONA. You?!

SISSY. Yes, me, Mona ... an' I gave him every
damn red-cent I had ... (*Gestures.*) there in my

purse to get him started ... someplace else ... away from you!

MONA. (*Charging at her.*) You are a disgustin', deceitful ... (*Slapping at* SISSY. *A crazed woman.*) Hypocrit ... claiming all these years to be my friend. He was none of your Goddamn business. (JOANNE *tries to pull her off* SISSY.) ... putting crazy ideas like that into the head of a helpless moron.

SISSY. He is not a moron, Goddammit!

MONA. (*Simply to* JOANNE.) Take your hands off me. (*To* SISSY.) You should be arrested an' locked up.

SISSY. Mona, dammit ... there is nothin' wrong with that boy.

MONA. (*Covers her ears.*) Lies! ... lies, nothin' but lies! All those doctors ... those doctors said he was a ...

SISSY. (*Prying her hands away from her ears.*) You never took him to no doctors ... he told me so!

MONA. He's lyin' ... He doesn't know the truth.

SISSY. And neither do you anymore, Mona. Where the hell did you get the idea anyhow? ... Did you see it in some movie, or did it jump out at you from the pages of some damn novel-of-the-month?

MONA. I am his mother and I know what he is! I don't believe one word you have just said ... This is a trick isn't it? (*Gestures to* JOANNE.) The two of you got together, didn't you? ... Got together to trick me into sayin' ... sayin' ...

SISSY. Sayin' what, Mona? ... That he isn't the son of James Dean? ... Hell, we've all known that for years ... everybody's known it, an' accepted it, but you.

MONA. He needs me!

SISSY. Not anymore, he doesn't. You tried to make him helpless an' dependent on you to keep him to yourself ... to keep James Dean alive ... (*Pleading.*) Let him go, for Chrissake.

MONA. (*Reaching for breath.*) I knew it would come to this in time. I could feel it inside me ...I had a premonition.

SISSY. You had gas.

MONA. (*A cornered child.*) I don't know why you have done this. We were friends ... I gave up a formal college education just to come back here ... (*Starts to wheeze.*) so we could ... could be together ... my pills, Sissy, get me my ...

SISSY. That asthma of yours is as phony as my rubber tits an' you know it.

EDNA. (*Rushing to* MONA.) Give her her pills ... hurry before she dies.

SISSY. She's not gonna die, for Chrissake.

EDNA. You leave her alone. She can die if she wants to. Mona, where's your pills? I'll get them for you.

MONA. (*Desperately trying to hold on to the little that is left.*) Thank you, but I'm breathin' better now. It's my heart, it sometimes skips a beat, especially on days like today when it's so hot ... an' dry. That long hot bus ride from Marfa didn't help matters none, either ... Edna Louise, did I show you the beautiful piece of Reata that I managed to retrieve from the destruction? (*Picks it up.*) It's not as easily identifiable as some of those I found in the past, but next year ... next year ... (*After a pause, pathetically to* SISSY.) They all know?

SISSY. Yes, we know.

MONA. All these years? (SISSY *nods "yes."*) How ... how embarrassing ... I ... I feel like such ... such a fool. (*Uneasy laugh.*)

JUANITA. There's no need to. Nobody's even thought about it ... or mentioned it, in years. He's just ... just Jimmy Dean, that's all. A normal, young ... man. (SHE *smiles.*)

MONA. I just wanted them all to notice me ... like when I was in "Giant" ... I was chosen ... for the first time in my life, I was chosen.

JOANNE. I chose you, Mona, I loved you.

MONA. They never would have believed it was you.

JOANNE. They never believed it was James Dean, either.

STELLA. Hey, wait a minute ... you mean it was really you on the front porch of Reata that night?

JOANNE. (SHE *nods.*) ... pretending I was James Dean.

STELLA. Holy shit! (*Quickly to* SISSY.) Sissy ... Sissy, did you know?

SISSY. (*Laughs.*) For Chrissake, Stella, all ya had to do was add it up.

STELLA. Wait'll Jimmy Dean finds out his daddy's really a lady ...

(*Distand thunder.* JOANNE *moves to the counter.* SISSY *stops her as* SHE *passes.*)

SISSY. You son-of-a-bitch! (*Smiles.*) Can I buy

you a drink? (*They move to the counter together.*)

JUANITA. Listen ... That storm's just passed right on over our heads, like we didn't even matter ... prob'ly on to some town that don't even need it. Believin' is so funny, ain't it? ... When what you're believin' in doesn't even know you exist ... all my life I prayed to Him, believed in Him ...

SISSY. It's the prayin' that did it.

JUANITA. (*Picks up the bourbon bottle.*) Does this really make things different?

JOANNE. Not a bit.

SISSY. Go on an' take a swig, Juanita. (SHE *pulls the string on the "Last Supper."*) ... God's not lookin'.

JUANITA. Sidney said it did. I tried to protect him. I even lied to God so's he'd take him into heaven. Maybe that's why God has punished me. He prob'ly found out the truth about Sidney.

SISSY. Well, looks like it's all over, don't it? ... beers gone, sandwiches are stale.

EDNA. It's so sad. I'm gonna cry, I just know it.

STELLA. Oh, for Chrissake.

EDNA. Aren't you sad, too? You must be at least a little sad

STELLA. All right, I'm sad ... you happy now? Come on, gather your crap together an' let's shove off before one of them gets the idea of startin' in on me next.

(EDNA *exits to gather her things.*)

SISSY. (*Laughs.*) You got somethin' hidden away

in your closet, Stella?

STELLA. (*Laughs back.*) Me?! ... only secret I've got is the combination to my safety deposit box.

SISSY. Then what's your big hurry? Hey, why not spend a day or two? ... Whattaya say?

STELLA. No, Merle don't like it when I stay away for long. (*Laughs.*) You know, I think the bastard's scared I'm gonna find somebody better.

EDNA. (*Entering.*) Well, goodbye everybody. I had such a very nice time. (*Starts to cry.*) I want to thank you all for still likin' me an' bein' nice to me although I'm not very smart. (*To* JOANNE.) Am I still glowin'?

JOANNE. Just like a Texas sunrise.

(EDNA *beams.*)

STELLA. (*To* EDNA.) C'mon.

SISSY. Goodbye, Stella. I'll see you in hell.

EDNA. It's not goodbye forever, I hope. We'll all get together sometime soon, won't we?

JOANNE. Shall we make a pact? Twenty years from tonight?

EDNA. (*Excited.*) Oh yea, let's ... won't that be excitin' to look forward to?

STELLA. Next time let's pick someplace cool, huh?

EDNA. We could have it at my house ... we've got us a window air-conditioner now ... an' the kids will be all grown up by then.

STELLA. Honey, at the rate you're going', you'll have seven more to replace 'em with, too. (*To* SISSY) Can ya imagine anythin' more horrible? (*Laughs.*)

SISSY. Stella, you'd give up everythin' you have

for just one of her kids, an' you know it.

STELLA. Me an' Merle's got kids...hundreds of 'em.

SISSY. Oil wells.

STELLA. They're our kids. We've got us a name for each one, too ... Let's see now ... there's Merle, Jr ... Freddie ... Stella Ann ...

EDNA. But a real one... You don't have a real one.

STELLA. Wouldn't have one in the house. Merle says the only way to have a baby is with beans an' potato salad at a barbecue. (*Laughs.*) He's such a card.

EDNA. I feel sorry for you.

STELLA. Sorry for me? Who the hell are you to feel sorry for me?

EDNA. (*Simply.*) Edna Louise Johnson.

STELLA. An' who the hell is that?

EDNA. Somebody very important to me an' my family. We maybe don't have lots of money an' belong to fancy country clubs...but we're happy with each other.

STELLA. Happy?! Christ, anybody can be happy. Look at me. I laugh my ass off all the time ... laugh at just about anythin'.

EDNA. But you're not happy.

STELLA. (*Angrily.*) I'm happy, Goddammit! (*A brief pause of embarrassment.* SISSY *starts to laugh. Then lightly.*) I never could stand people who say they have to go, then never do. (SHE *grabs* EDNA *and drags her out.*)

JUANITA. (*To* MONA.) You'll lock up an' turn off the lights when you leave now. (*To* SISSY.) An' I want to see you first thing in the mornin' takin' down them decorations. (*Removing her apron, gathering her purse, etc.* MONA (THEN) *enters the front door.*) I'm gonna stop on over to the graveyard before goin' on home an' have myself a little talk with Sidney. I'll see you in the mornin', Mona... same time as always?

MONA (THEN. I'll be here, Juanita.

(JUANITA *starts to exit.*)

JOANNE. It was nice to see you again, Juanita.

JUANITA. (*Turns to her.*) I hope you found what you came in here lookin' for... Miss. (SHE *exits.* MONA *follows her to the door.*)

SISSY. Well I guess it's all over now... but the end.

JOANNE. How's it end?

SISSY. (*A glance to* MONA *at the door.*) With just us, I guess... same as it started.

(JOE *appears at the door with a suitcase.* HE *has changed clothes.*)

JOE. I came by to say so long, to Sissy.

MONA (THEN). She had herself a date over to the graveyard with Lester T.

JOE. (*Smiles.*) Tell her goodbye for me then, will ya? (*Starts to go.*)

MONA (THEN). Where you goin'... do you know?

JOE. Do you care?

MONA (THEN). I had to, Joe... will you ever forgive me?

JOE. (*A pause and then flatly.*) No. (HE *turns and exits.*)

SISSY. Don't worry none about your car... There's

a bus leavin' from Big Spring at nine-thirty. He just borrowed it to get there in time to catch it, I'm sure.

JOANNE. Where's he going from there?

SISSY. To see where all the trains go. (MONA *re-enters from outside as* MONA (THEN) *goes to the backroom for her suitcase.*) Hey, how about the McGuire Sisters gettin' together for one final number ... for ol' time's sake. Whattaya say?

JOANNE. I don't think I even remember the words anymore.

SISSY. Hell, I never knew the words. Just make your mouth move an' pretend ya do. C'mon, Mona.

MONA. (*Goes to the phone and tries it one final time.*) He's really gone?

SISSY. He promised me that he'd write a letter an' let you know where he ends up.

MONA. I'll be worryin' about him all the time.

SISSY. He's gonna do just fine, Mona.

MONA. I'm his mother. I need to worry.

SISSY. (*Simply.*) I know.

JOANNE. (*Holds her hand out to* MONA.) C'mon, Mona ... let's forgive and forget.

MONA. (*After a pause, smiles and takes her hand.* It's been so long, I don't know if I was on the left or the right.

(*The musical introduction to the McGuire Sisters' recording of "Sincerely," comes up.* MONA (THEN) *enters from the backroom with her suitcase.* SHE *looks around the store, goes to a photo of James Dean and kisses it, then goes to the front door.*)

SISSY. You were on the right, Joe was on the left, an' I was dead center.

JOANNE. Sissy, your center was never dead. (THEY *all laugh.*)

MONA. Come on, we need to be serious.

JOANNE. Remember how we dressed up alike in those awful blue dresses?

MONA. I thought those dresses were pretty.

SISSY. All right ... here it comes now ... ready?

(*The vocal begins as* THEY *sing along to the record. Occassionally* THEY *lose their words and start to laugh.* MONA (THEN) *goes to the front door, turns and almost as if* SHE *sees them, smiles. The lights slowly fade to black.*)

COSTUME PLOT

MONA:
>blue cotton shirtwaist dress
>low heeled, off-white sandals
>watch

JUANITA:
>print cotton housedress
>print bib apron
>low sandals

MONA (THEN):
>blue print school dress
>white socks
>saddle shoes
>"Disciples" jacket

SISSY:
>flashy dress (above the knee)
>high heeled sandals
>hose
>heavy jewelry
>padded bra

SISSY (THEN):
>peasant blouse
>short skating skirt
>hose
>black flat shoes

padded bra
"Disciples" jacket

JOE:
faded bib overalls
faded short-sleeved sport shirt
high top black tennis shoes
"Disciples" jacket
END:
worn corduroy pants
sport shirt
worn corduroy jacket (not matching)
same tennis shoes

EDNA LOUISE:
dirty white beautician's dress (to show off pregnancy)
white socks
low white nurse shoes
CHANGE TO:
fancy party dress (tight across the front and unzipped in back)
high heeled sandals
"Disciples" jacket

JOANNE:
white linen suit
beige simple blouse
high heeled sandals
hose
long head scarf
sunglasses
shoulder bag

PROPERTY LIST

LUNCH COUNTER:
    Orange Crush Machine
    stemmed cake tray with lid and doughnuts
    3 pr. salt and pepper shakers
    3 sugars
3 menus in holders
fly swatter (JUANITA)
    3 napkin holders
  UNDERNEATH:
    1 dozen coke glasses
    silverware in tray
    stack or plates

BEHIND:
  SHELF WITH:
    hotplate
    radio
    plates
    cups saucers
    pots pans
    soup cans
    purse (JUANITA)
  ON WALL:
    electric "Last Supper"
    menu
    Alka Seltzer display
    Orange Crush ad

IN FRONT:
> 4 swivel stools
> 2 small pedestal tables with napkins holders and
>   salt & pepper shakers
> 3 chairs at each table
> broom
> wall telephone
> magazine rack with bench in front
> gumball machine with red gumball (PRESET)
> ladder
> box of decorations

SHRINETABLE:
> 15 various sized framed photos of James Dean
> large photo of James Dean outlined in Christmas
>   tree lights
> framed photo of "Disciples of James Dean"
> gold plaque

COSMETIC DISPLAY RACK WITH:
> nailpolish (SISSY)
> lipstick, rouge, eyebrow pencils (SISSY (THEN))

SUNGLASSES DISPLAY

BACK ROOM:
> shelves of merchandise
> 2 wooden crates (SITTABLE)

OUTSIDE FRONT DOORS:
> beat up weekender suitcase (MONA)
> piece of Reata inside

paperback copy of "Gone With The Wind" (MO-
NA)
handerchief (MONA)
purse with asthma pills (MONA)
case of "Lone Star" beer (SISSY)
bag of groceries (SISSY) ;
  sandwich meat
  mayonnaise
  potato chips

NEWSPAPER (Odessa-American) (SISSY)
WEEKENDER SUITCASE (MONA (THEN))
LOAF OF BREAD (JUANITA)
PLASTIC CLEANERS BAG WITH PARTY DRESS
    (EDNA)
LARGE PURSE WITH BOTTLE OF BOURBON
    AND 8x10 NUDE PHOTO OF DEAN
        (STELLA)
PURSE WITH NOTEBOOK (EDNA)
PURSE WITH CIGARETTES (SISSY)
PURSE WITH CIGARETTES (SISSY)
SMALL SUITCASE (JOE)

FROM BACK ROOM:
  boxes of cosmetics (SISSY (THEN))
  10 magazines (SISSY (THEN))
  6 bottles of "Lone Star" (SISSY (THEN))
  Mona's club jacket (JOE)
  lace handerchief with matchbook
      (MONA (THEN))
  James Dean magazine (MONA (THEN))
  cigarette butt (JOE)
  cigarettes (SISSY (THEN))

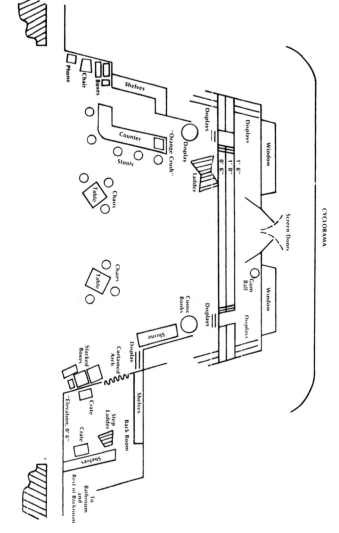

"COME BACK TO THE 5 AND DIME, JIMMY DEAN, JIMMY DEAN"

CYCLORAMA

Phone
Chair
Boxes
Shelves
Displays
Displays
Window
Display
Counter
"Orange Crush"
Display
Ladder
Stools
Chairs
Table
1' 0"
0' 6"
1' 6"
Screen Doors
Chairs
Table
Gum Ball
Window
Displays
Comic Books
Displays
Shrine
Display
Curtained Arch
Shelves
Back Room
Stacked Boxes
Step Ladder
Crate
"Elevation, 0' 6""
Crate
Shelves
To Bathroom and Rest of Backroom

Scale 1/8"   1' 0"

COCKEYED
William Missouri Downs

Comedy / 3m, 1f / Unit Set

Phil, an average nice guy, is madly in love with the beautiful Sophia. The only problem is that she's unaware of his existence. He tries to introduce himself but she looks right through him. When Phil discovers Sophia has a glass eye, he thinks that might be the problem, but soon realizes that she really can't see him. Perhaps he is caught in a philosophical hyperspace or dualistic reality or perhaps beautiful women are just unaware of nice guys. Armed only with a B.A. in philosophy, Phil sets out to prove his existence and win Sophia's heart. This fast moving farce is the winner of the HotCity Theatre's GreenHouse New Play Festival. The St. Louis Post-Dispatch called Cockeyed a clever romantic comedy, Talkin' Broadway called it "hilarious," while Playback Magazine said that it was "fresh and invigorating."

Winner!
of the HotCity Theatre GreenHouse New Play Festival

"Rocking with laughter...hilarious...polished and engaging work draws heavily on the age-old conventions of farce: improbable situations, exaggerated characters, amazing coincidences, absurd misunderstandings, people hiding in closets and barely missing each other as they run in and out of doors...full of comic momentum as Cockeyed hurtles toward its conclusion."
- Talkin' Broadway